exposed

exposed

a twisted cedars mystery

C.J. Carmichael

TULE
PUBLISHING

Exposed

Copyright© 2016 Carla Daum
Tule Publishing First Printing, July 2024

The Tule Publishing, Inc.

ALL RIGHTS RESERVED

First Publication by Tule Publishing 2024

Cover design by Croco Designs

No part of this book may be used or reproduced in any manner whatsoever without written permission except in the case of brief quotations embodied in critical articles and reviews.

This is a work of fiction. Names, characters, places, and incidents are products of the author's imagination or are used fictitiously. Any resemblance to actual events, locales, organizations, or persons, living or dead, is entirely coincidental.

AI was not used to create any part of this book and no part of this book may be used for generative training.

ISBN: 978-1-964703-09-1

The root of the modern day library goes back to the United Kingdom and 1847 when Parliament appointed a committee, led by William Ewart, to consider the necessity of establishing, throughout the nation, free libraries, assessable by all.

– per Michael H. Harris in *The History of Libraries in the Western World*

※

During the post-Civil War years in the United States, the establishment of public libraries was spearheaded chiefly by women's clubs. They contributed their own collections of books, conducted lengthy fund raising campaigns for buildings, and lobbied within their communities for financial support for libraries.

– per Paula D. Watson, in *Library Quarterly*

※

A truly great library contains something in it to offend everyone.

– Jo Godwin

※

Libraries…
are the collective memory of the human race.

– Donald C. Davis, Jr.

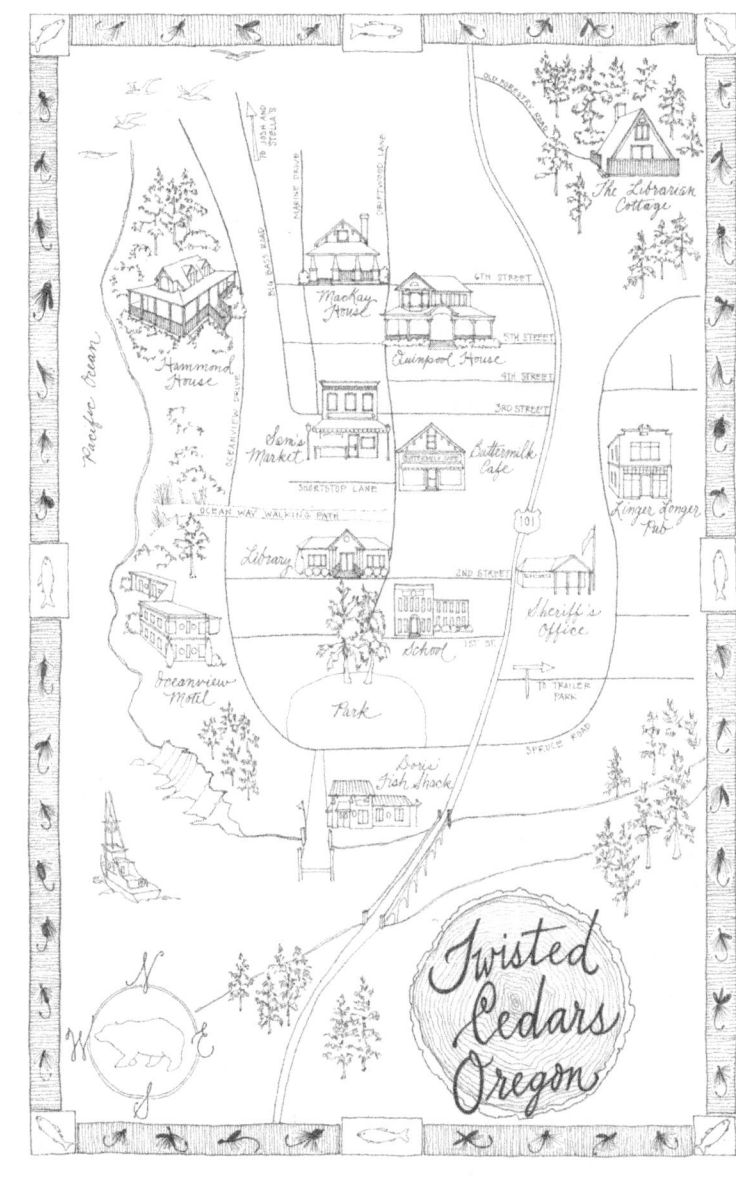

families of twisted cedars

The Lachlans

Katie: Married Ed Lachlan and had two children, Dougal and Jamie. After her divorce she supported her kids by working as a cleaning woman with her partner and friend, Stella Ward. At the age of 55 Katie died of cancer.

Edward (Ed): Former husband of Katie, and father of Dougal and Jamie. Remarried to Crystal Halloway and had daughter, Emma. Killed Crystal during a domestic dispute and served time in Oregon penitentiary. Upon release six months ago, he skipped parole and his official whereabouts is unknown.

Dougal: 34-year-old son of Katie and Ed, brother to Jamie. He played high school football with Wade McKay and Kyle Quinpool. At 18 he moved to New York City and began a career writing true crime novels.

Jamie: 28-year-old daughter of Katie and Ed, sister to Dougal. She is a CPA and works for a local accounting firm. She recently married Kyle Quinpool who has two children from a previous marriage.

The Hammonds

Jonathan: Former town mayor died two years ago in car crash with his wife. Daughters: Daisy and Charlotte.

Patricia: Jonathan's wife, mother of Daisy and Charlotte. Killed with her husband in a car crash.

Shirley: Jonathan's sister was the local town librarian before she was found hanged to death in the basement of the library when she was 41-years-old. Her death was ruled suicide. Never married, she lived in a cottage in the forest, five miles from town, which came to be known locally as the Librarian Cottage.

Daisy: Daughter of Jonathan and Patricia, Kyle Quinpool's first wife and mother to twins, Cory and Chester. She disappeared shortly after her divorce and hasn't been heard from since.

Charlotte: 28-year-old adopted daughter of Jonathan and Patricia. She works as head librarian in Twisted Cedars.

The MacKays

Grant: Father to Wade and husband of Allison, he was the Sheriff of Curry County for over thirty years.

Allison: Mother to Wade and wife of Grant. She was a piano teacher until she and her husband retired to Arizona.

Wade: 34-year-old son of Grant and Allison, he was high

school buddies with Dougal Lachlan, Kyle Quinpool, and Daisy Hammond. Worked as deputy in Umatilla County before returning to Twisted Cedars and being elected as Sheriff of Curry County.

The Quinpools

Jim: Wealthiest man in town. He owns the local real estate business, Quinpool Realty. He and his wife Muriel had one son, Kyle. He and Muriel recently divorced.

Muriel: Wife of Jim and mother to Kyle, she and her husband moved in with Kyle after he divorced his wife, Daisy. Muriel became the twins' primary caregiver. A year ago she divorced Jim and moved away from Twisted Cedars.

Kyle: Son of Jim and Muriel, he works with his father at Quinpool Realty. He had twins, Cory and Chester with his first wife, Daisy, and subsequently married Jamie Lachlan.

Cory: 9-year-old daughter of Kyle and Daisy and twin sister to Chester.

Chester: 9-year-old son of Kyle and Daisy and twin brother to Cory.

chapter one

CHARLOTTE HAMMOND HAD been legal guardian of her dead sister's children, nine-year-old twins Chester and Cory Quinpool, for less than two months when her worst nightmare came true.

It happened in September, the first week of the new school term. The twins had started fourth grade, time was marching on, and they'd be turning ten this November.

No doubt the past year would be one they'd happily put behind them. Only that summer they'd found out their mentally ill mother—Charlotte's sister, Daisy—hadn't deserted them as originally thought but instead had been killed and illegally buried near an old family cottage.

Less than a month after that shocker, their father, Kyle Quinpool, had been arrested on charges of fraud and criminally negligent homicide. Rather than put his children through the stress of a trial—or so he'd claimed—he'd chosen to plead guilty and serve his sentence.

So…it had been a tough summer.

And now Chester had gone missing somewhere between school and the babysitter's house. The disappearance began with only a mildly concerning phone call from Nola Thompson, the woman who was supposed to be minding the twins for the hour and a half between school and the closing of the public library where Charlotte worked.

"All the kids have been home for fifteen minutes," Nola said without preamble. "Still no sign of Chester."

Charlotte began closing windows on her computer. Her nephew had ridden his bike today, so if anything, he should have made it to the Thompson house first. "Does Cory know where he is?"

"Nope. Anyway, if he made plans to go to one of his friend's houses, *I'm* the one who needs to be told. I have enough on my hands without worrying about him." Nola sounded more annoyed than worried.

"He didn't say anything about his plans to me, either," Charlotte admitted, getting up from her desk and moving down the mystery aisle so Zoey, shelving books just a few feet from Charlotte's desk, wouldn't hear.

Zoey made a perfectly fine librarian assistant, but since Charlotte had taken custody of the twins, the married mother of three made a point of second-guessing every parenting decision Charlotte made. Given her experience, Zoey probably felt entitled. But Charlotte had seen Zoey with her children, and her hardline approach was not one Charlotte wanted to emulate.

"He's getting to be a real handful," Nola continued, and Charlotte knew it was true.

Earlier that summer she'd sent the kids back to summer camp so they could avoid the local gossip about their parents. But now that school was in session, she couldn't protect them anymore. Cory reacted to the teasing and bullying by being super sweet and accommodating—as if she had to apologize and atone for every one of her parents' sins.

Chester, on the other hand, retaliated with his fists.

Complicating the situation, Nola's oldest child, Bruce, was among the worst of the bullies, so he and Chester were always at odds.

"I'll go looking for him," Charlotte said. "Meanwhile, if he does show up please call me right away."

"Fine. But this is the last straw. I'm not going to be able to provide after-school care for Chester anymore. Cory, yes. She's an angel. But that brother of hers…"

"Got it." If she sounded short, Charlotte didn't care. It was past time she made alternate arrangements for the twins. Nola Thompson had never been intended to be more than a stopgap solution.

Charlotte grabbed her purse from the bottom drawer of her desk, aware of Zoey hovering nearby.

"I have to leave early. Do you mind locking up?" Charlotte hated to ask the favor, as she knew Zoey would take this as yet another sign of her parental incompetency.

"Sure. Is it Chester again? If you ask me, that boy is going to turn out just like his father unless you take a firm hand."

Charlotte didn't answer, just made her way outside.

She didn't believe Zoey had the answer for how to deal with Chester. But neither did she. Single and twenty-eight years old, Charlotte was learning how to parent on the fly.

If the twins had been younger, she might have been more equipped. She had no trouble connecting with the three- and four-year-olds who attended her preschool reading circle every week.

But she had less experience with older children. Her boyfriend, true-crime writer Dougal Lachlan, was even more hopeless.

Not that she'd seen much of him lately. Since the twins had moved in, he'd become increasingly reclusive. Given the issues he had with his own father, she guessed he wasn't keen on stepping into any sort of parental role himself.

Or maybe he was just getting tired of her.

Outside Charlotte slipped on her sunglasses. September was often one of the nicest weather months for coastal Oregon, and today was a perfect example. Sunny, hot, almost no wind. Since she lived only a few blocks from the library she never drove to work, which meant she had to walk home to get her car. She hurried along the Ocean Way walking path, barely managing a smile as she passed by the mother of one of her favorite teenaged patrons.

When she reached the gracious three-story home where she'd grown up, her first instinct was to check the garage for Chester's bike. It wasn't there. She went through the mudroom into the house.

"Chester? Are you home?" She ran through the entire house, checking every room, including the bedroom that had once been Daisy's and was now the twins'. She suspected Chester had agreed to share the room with his sister because he knew she was afraid to be alone.

What would Cory do if they didn't find her brother? If he—?

No. She couldn't let herself think that way.

After she'd searched the house, Charlotte checked the yard, then the beach that stretched out on either side of her property. It was deserted.

Where else would he go? He hadn't been keen on hanging out with his friends lately. Maybe the park by the school? Or the public beach?

Surely he wouldn't dare go near the bluffs...?

Fear slammed into her, causing her to freeze in one instant, then start running to her car the next.

Charlotte backed out of the driveway, shifted gears, then hit the gas a little too hard, throwing up bits of gravel and causing her body to lurch forward, then abruptly back. She gripped the steering wheel like it was a throw line and she was a drowning swimmer, and pushed her speed beyond the town limit.

In less than thirty seconds she was at the park. The manicured green space led to a public beach on the other side of the sand dunes. Closer to the main road, screened off by shrubbery and a chain-link fence from the danger of traffic, the ocean, and the bluffs was a playground. The children clambering on the monkey bars and swings were all much younger than Chester, but Charlotte approached one of the mothers sitting on a nearby bench who was scrolling on her mobile phone.

"Hi! I'm looking for my nephew. He's nine years old, sandy-colored hair, and wearing a dark green T-shirt and jeans. Have you seen anyone like that?"

The woman, who was cute and looked twenty, if that, gave her a blank stare. Then she shook her head. "Sorry. I haven't."

"Right. Thanks anyway." Charlotte dashed through a gate to the dunes to check the beach next. Though going near the ocean without adult supervision was strictly forbidden, at this point she would have been relieved to spot Chester on the expansive sandy shoreline.

Quickly she scanned the scattering of people out enjoying the beautiful day. No children close to Chester's age here, either. She stopped to ask a mother of toddlers if she'd seen anyone who looked like her nephew.

"We've been here for over an hour, and there's been no one like that," the young mom said.

God. Where was he?

Her gaze flashed up to the bluffs. All she could see were trees. Knowing it was possible Chester was purposefully hiding, she attacked the steep incline, taking longer than she wanted to finally gain the summit.

But Chester wasn't here, either.

Terrible possibilities swamped her mind. Had he been hurt or worse in a terrible accident? Been approached by a sick child molester?

No. Please no.

Charlotte skidded and slid her way down from the bluffs.

There were still other places to look.

She'd start at the school. It seemed doubtful he was still there, but she ought to check. Plus she needed a list of his classmates. Perhaps Nola was right and he'd gone home with one of the other kids.

Since the school was only a short walk from the park, Charlotte didn't bother with her car. She ran across the road, her pulse a loud, rapid-fire beat above the rasping of her breathing. She grasped and tugged at the main doors, only to find they were locked.

She left the paved sidewalk and jogged across the freshly mown lawn that ran down the side of the three-story brick structure, hoping for an open window and someone nearby to hear her call out.

Within seconds she heard the faint sound of a woman speaking, her tone lecturing, though no words were distinguishable. Charlotte traced the sound to an open window, which she guessed—having spent a lot of time in the school the past two weeks—was the staff room.

"Hello!" She was tall and had no trouble looking into the window. About eight women and a couple of men were seated throughout a room furnished with two round tables, a sofa, and several armchairs. "I'm sorry to interrupt, but my nephew, Chester Quinpool, didn't come home from school today."

As she spoke, she focused one by one on the teachers' faces. Most were familiar to her. The school lacked funding for a proper library and so often made use of the public one which was, after all, only a ten-minute walk away.

"Charlotte?" Olivia Young, the twins' teacher, came to the window. "Weren't Cory and Chester supposed to go to the Thompsons' after school today?"

Olivia was in her early thirties, newly married, and, if Charlotte wasn't mistaken, newly pregnant as well. They'd had several meetings already to discuss the twins and how to best help them transition into the new school year after the trauma of having their father imprisoned for their mother's homicide.

"Cory did. But Chester still hasn't shown up." Charlotte glanced at her phone to make sure she hadn't missed an update from Nola. "I've looked for him at home, at the park, and the beach. I even climbed up the bluffs, but I've seen no sign of him."

The school principal, Gabrielle Hodges, an athletic, handsome woman in her late fifties, stepped closer to the window. Gabrielle had been Charlotte's fourth-grade teacher way back when, and she had a comforting aura of authority as she weighed in. "I'm sure we'll find him, Charlotte. We'll search the school thoroughly and call all his classmates. There's a good chance he went home to play with one of them."

"Maybe." But Chester hadn't seemed to be on good terms with any of the other children these days. This past week he'd been spending most of his free time alone in his bedroom.

"Why don't you come inside?" Gabrielle invited. "I'll go unlock the front door for you."

"I have to keep looking for Chester."

"Okay. You do that. We'll make sure he isn't hiding somewhere on school property."

"And I'll call everyone on the class list," Olivia promised.

"Thank you." Focusing on Olivia, she added, "Can you think of any incident that came up today, something involving Chester, that might help explain where he's gone?"

Olivia's brow furrowed. "He did seem troubled. But I'm afraid that's not unusual."

No, sadly, it was not.

"I don't want to alarm you," Gabrielle said. "He's probably gone to a friend's house or something. But I'm going to call 911."

Adrenaline jolted through Charlotte's system, tightening every muscle while turning her stomach—and her world—upside down. Alerting the authorities elevated the situation from worrisome to catastrophic. Possibilities that had seemed remote at first, possibilities like an accident or a kidnapping, could no longer be pushed to the back of her mind.

She glanced at her watch. Chester had now been missing for forty minutes.

"Yes. Call 911."

Charlotte left her cell phone number with them, then jogged back to the sidewalk, trying to push through her panic and think rationally.

Though it was a possibility that had to be crossed off the list, she didn't think they'd find Chester hiding on school property or at one of his classmates' homes. Where else could she look?

She supposed she could randomly drive up and down the main streets of town in the hopes of spotting him or his bike.

Then inspiration struck. Maybe Chester had gone to see his grandfather, Jim Quinpool. For a few years Jim and Muriel had lived with Kyle and the twins. If Chester was upset, his grandfather was an obvious person to run to.

As she hurried back to her car, she called Jim. The phone rang and rang on the other end, but there was no answer. That didn't mean Jim wasn't home. He'd wanted custody of the twins after his son went to prison, and he'd been ticked off when the court appointed her instead. Possibly he'd seen her name on the call display and had refused to answer out of spite.

So she'd just have to go flush him out. On the drive to

Jim's place—he now lived in an apartment above the Realtor business he'd once run with Kyle—she tried Wade McKay, the Curry County sheriff and a personal friend.

The 911 call would be routed through his office. But she wanted to speak to him personally.

Wade answered after the first ring. "Charlotte. We just got the call from Gabrielle Hodges. Where are you?"

"In my car, on my way to J-Jim's house." She swallowed. At the first sound of Wade's voice, she'd had a sudden urge to cry.

But she couldn't break down now. She had to be strong and hope for the best—that she would find Chester soon and he'd be fine.

"I've already checked the park across from the school and the beach. Chester's teacher is calling everyone in his class, and the rest of the staff are searching the school."

"That's good. Drive carefully, Charlotte. Try to stay calm. I'm sending out every available vehicle to comb this town. Chances are good we'll find him in the next half an hour or so."

Even as he said that, Charlotte passed a black and white SUV with SHERIFF CURRY COUNTY stenciled on the side panel. The driver, Deputy Dunne, gave her a wave and a nod, as if to say, *Don't worry, ma'am. We're on this.*

Before Dougal moved back to Twisted Cedars, she and Wade had dated. He'd even asked her to marry him once—though she was pretty sure he hadn't loved her at the time. For sure he didn't love her now. But she was grateful he wasn't the sort of man to hold a grudge.

"Thanks, Wade. I just—thank you."

"Of course. We'll be in touch."

Charlotte ended the call but kept a tight hold on her phone. *Please ring. Please be Nola, reporting that Chester has finally shown up. Or Olivia, saying Chester is fine, he'd gone home with a school friend...*

But her phone remained silent.

She wished desperately that she had a way to reach Chester directly. The twins owned iPads, which they weren't allowed to bring to school. But they didn't have phones. Their father had said they had to wait until they turned thirteen—a rule that had seemed reasonable to Charlotte once.

Now she swore that as soon as they found Chester, she would go out and get them not just phones but possibly GPS tracking devices she'd strap to their ankles.

Charlotte turned onto Driftwood Lane, the town's main drag, grateful that August was over and there was plenty of available parking. She was able to pull into a space right outside Quinpool Realty. The business was closed. It had been since Kyle's arrest.

She rushed out of her car, glancing around, hoping to see if not Chester, then at least his bike. But neither one was in sight. She opened the door to the left of the glass door to Quinpool Realty and then climbed a narrow, steep flight of stairs to the upper apartment.

With each step her heart thumped harder. Sweat rose on her hands, filming against the phone and keys she was carrying. She put both into her pockets, then rubbed her palms on the light wool blend of her skirt.

At the top of the stairs was a small landing and a wooden

door with a peephole and a slot for mail. She listened, straining for the sound of Chester's voice within, but all she could hear was the faint drone of a television.

She rapped on the door, waiting less than ten seconds before repeating.

"Jim?" she called out. "It's Charlotte. I'm looking for Chester."

Finally he opened. Behind him was a dimly lit room with a sofa and television. The room had a foul, stale, alcoholic odor. And so did Jim.

He looked rough. Unshaven, clothes rumpled as if he'd slept in them—for more than one night, hair that had gone too long without a wash or a cut. Considering he'd been one of the better dressed men in town once, it was a long fall.

The man obviously needed help, but she couldn't worry about that right now.

"Is Chester here?" She scanned the room as she asked this. When she tried to step forward, Jim blocked her.

"No, he isn't. What the hell is going on?"

Charlotte wished she had an answer for him. She would have given anything to see her nephew sitting on that disgusting couch, eating junk food and watching sitcom reruns with his grandfather.

But he wasn't here.

He wasn't at Nola's or at home or the school or the park or any of the normal places he liked to hang out.

So where was he?

Charlotte's mind went blank as a terrible fear took grip of her body and soul.

Dougal had warned her that the horror that had gripped

their town the past few months wasn't over. Kyle Quinpool may have been arrested. Her sister's death was being avenged. But there was a bigger evil lurking in Twisted Cedars.

She didn't want to believe it. But it seemed there was a very good chance Chester's disappearance was linked to that.

chapter two

"Are you sure this is the right place?"

Jamie Lachlan didn't answer her brother's question. Instead, she slid out of the passenger side of his SUV into tall wild grass that tickled the backs of her calves exposed by her capri jeans.

They were at the far end of a gravel road that followed the Elk River into the Grassy Knob Wilderness. All around were giant trees, wild grasses, and tangles of vine maples. The last sign of civilization, a rundown cabin, had been a few miles back. Even cell-phone coverage didn't reach this far.

"Jamie? Is this the place?"

She heard the driver's-side door slam shut and the sound of his footsteps swishing through the grass. But she couldn't stop staring at the two-story home in front of her.

About a month ago she'd met a man here. Brian Greenway had contacted the CPA firm where she worked looking for tax advice for his extensive investment portfolio. The amount of money involved had been significant enough that her bosses had sent her out here to meet him—and get his signature on a letter of engagement.

She'd been so excited at the time. Being sent to sign up a new client—especially an important new client like Brian

Greenway—seemed to be, had felt like a vote of confidence in her work. Not to mention an indicator that one day she would be invited to be a partner at Howard & Mason.

But shortly after she'd obtained Greenway's John Henry, he'd disappeared.

According to the property management firm that handled this place, rent was paid up for six months. They had no idea Greenway wasn't using the place anymore.

But he so obviously wasn't.

Hard to believe that in just one month a property could come to look so neglected. But this one, with the overgrown lawn and curtained windows, did. All the patio furniture, including the stuff from the adjacent gazebo, was gone. As was the black pickup truck that had been parked here last time.

Only when Dougal put a hand on her shoulder did Jamie come out of her trance and remember his question.

"Yes. This is the place where I met with Brian Greenway."

Dougal's dark eyes narrowed. At thirty-four her brother had six years on her, and the gap had always been a distancing one. The years he'd spent working as a true-crime author in New York City hadn't made them any closer. Nor had his almost violent opposition to her marriage to Kyle Quinpool last June.

Time had proven Dougal right on that one, since Kyle was now in prison and their marriage was in the process of being annulled.

But that didn't mean he was right about *everything*.

Even as she had the thought, Jamie recognized the petulance behind it.

"Tell me what happened that day. Walk me through it."

She sighed, annoyed that he'd insisted on driving all this way when she'd already told him every detail three times over. Training her eyes on the front door, she recalled the heat of the July day when she'd been here last. A chickadee had been singing when she'd stepped out of her car. "I parked just about where you did now. Greenway came to the door a moment later."

"Describe him."

Since Dougal was walking toward the house, she followed so she wouldn't have to shout.

"He was an inch or two shorter than you. Slender. He looked about sixty, I'd say. His hair was gray and short. Oh, he had a beard—it looked freshly trimmed."

Dougal tried the main door, which was locked, then attempted to peer into the windows, but the curtains effectively blocked his view. "How about his eyes? Are you sure you didn't see them?"

"He wore sunglasses the entire time."

"You didn't get even a quick glance?"

"I've told you all of this already. Why do you insist on going over it and over it?"

Earlier that week Dougal had helped her settle into the new house she'd purchased on Horizon Hill Road. He'd moved her sofa from one wall to the other until she figured out where it looked best. He'd helped her connect her TV and internet and had shown her how to program the fancy thermostat for the gas furnace.

It was only because he'd been so nice that she'd finally

given in to his demand to show her this place and to go over—yet again—her encounter with Brian Greenway in July.

"I'm hoping you'll remember something—a detail, a sentence, a word—that will help me prove my theory." Dougal paused to look back at her. "I didn't complain when you made me move that heavy sofa to six different places before we pushed it back to the original spot, did I?"

"Fine. No, I didn't get even a glance at his eyes. He claimed he was very sensitive to the sun. He had his sunglasses on the whole time."

"What about his voice? Did it sound familiar?"

She paused. A breeze rippled through the grass, over her skin, through her hair. It had been dead calm the last time she was here. In her mind a voice echoed. *Call me Brian... Hope you didn't mind the drive.*

"I *did* have the feeling I'd heard his before. Which was strange because our meeting had been set up by Colin."

Dougal looked at her sharply. "Did it—sound like mine?"

She could feel the pain behind the question. Dougal begrudged any resemblance between himself and their father. And that was who he believed Brian Greenway really was. Their dad, Edward Lachlan, a man Jamie had never met—unless Dougal was correct and she'd spoken to him last July, in this very spot.

"Maybe. I'm not sure." When Dougal turned away in disappointment, she felt compelled to apologize. "I'm *sorry*. It was a while ago, okay?"

"I didn't mean to pressure you. What happened next?"

"He suggested we talk in the gazebo." She glanced at the cedar structure about thirty feet from the house.

"Let's check it out."

Again Jamie followed her brother, pausing as he opened the screen door. When the hinges screeched in protest, she couldn't remember if it had done so before. Inside cobwebs festooned the rafters like holiday garland and a layer of grit had settled on the plank flooring.

"There was a table here before. And cushioned chairs. He'd set out lemonade and snacks."

But now the space was empty. She traced a circle with her steps while Dougal stood and watched.

"What did you talk about?"

"He told me he'd been living here about a month, and then he asked a bunch of questions about my background, including where I'd gone to college. I thought he was vetting me to see if I was qualified to handle his tax returns."

Was it possible she'd been talking to her father that day without realizing it? Jamie found it almost impossible to believe she wouldn't have felt some sort of connection if it were true.

All her life people had been protecting her from Edward Lachlan. They told her he was a man with a dangerous temper, capable of great violence. It was why her mother, Katie, had kicked him out when she did, not even telling him she was pregnant with Jamie.

The idea was that he would never even know he had a daughter.

Years later, when Edward was imprisoned for killing his second wife, Katie's caution was vindicated.

Not exactly Daddy of the Year material.

And, according to Dougal, he'd done worse. Much worse.

"Did this *Greenway* actually show you his portfolio?"

She nodded.

"And is he wealthy?"

Again she nodded, wondering if by so doing she was breaking client confidentiality, if indeed Greenway could still be considered one. He'd paid a significant retainer, but he'd also stopped answering phone calls and emails shortly after her visit. If Dougal's theory was correct, his only purpose in approaching Howard & Mason had been to meet her. Now that he had, they'd never hear from him again.

Despite the warm air, she shivered. "We talked about some of his tax issues, and then he asked if I'd like to walk down to the river."

"And you said yes," Dougal continued, moving the script forward. "Show me where you went."

They left the gazebo, and as Jamie picked out the faint trail through the forest to the river, she remembered more trivia from that day. "He talked about the salmon spawning in the drainage of Dry Creek. I asked if he was a fisherman. He said he didn't have the patience."

The sound of rushing water grew louder as she made her way through the trees, her sandals crunching over small twigs and scattered pine cones. When she pushed aside the branch of a thick spruce tree, a squirrel came rushing down the trunk to scold her before dashing back to safety.

Jamie stopped when she came to the river bank. What a beautiful, magical place. The river spanned about twenty-five feet, disappearing from view as it curved to the right. "There's a big waterfall beyond that curve, but you have to walk along these rocks to see it."

The river was shallow on this bank, so clear you could see perfectly to the pebbled floor. As Jamie stepped cautiously from one big rock to the next, the chattering of the river became a dull roar. She stopped well back from the ledge where the land abruptly gave way to a twenty-foot drop.

Even as she was doing so, Dougal grabbed her arm. "Careful! You're too close to the edge."

"Brian Greenway warned me to be careful that day," she recalled. "I remember I leaned too far forward and almost lost my balance. But then he pulled me back."

That brief moment of physical contact between them—it had passed so quickly. She'd felt nothing, no special bond to suggest she was being touched by her father.

"Shit, Jamie. Are you sure he wasn't the reason you almost fell?"

She started to deny it, then stopped. Memory was a funny thing. Now that Dougal had planted the idea in her head, she almost believed that yes, it had happened that way.

"You're trembling. Let's sit down for a bit." Dougal pointed to a log a few yards back from the ledge.

Jamie sank down gratefully, stretching out her legs but folding her arms over her chest. Even from this distance she could feel a deliciously cool mist from the cascading river.

"If Brian Greenway was our father, why would he have pulled a stunt like that?"

"He meant it as a message for me." Dougal sat beside her, staring out at the river, his expression stony. "He killed our half sister, Joelle, and her baby for the same reason. He wants me to write a book about his killing spree in the seventies."

"Or else what—he'll kill me next?" She tried to sound incredulous. Because it was unbelievable. And yet so many awful things had happened the past four months.

When Dougal didn't respond, she had to concede. "Maybe you're right. God knows you were right about Kyle."

※

DOUGAL WAS THIRTY minutes into the drive back to Twisted Cedars with his sister when the phone he'd tossed into his cup holder let out a series of chirps.

Jamie's phone was doing the same thing.

"Guess we're back in cell-phone range." Jamie fished her phone out of her purse. A moment later she said, "Oh, crap. No. No way."

"What is it?" Foreboding, cold as a rogue wave in December, washed over him. The call could be about anything. Maybe she'd missed an important meeting at work. But his fear was confirmed with her next words.

"It's Chester. He's missing."

Icy fear slid down Dougal's spine. He tried to push it away with reason. Kids broke rules sometimes. Maybe that was all this was. "How long? Fifteen minutes? Half an hour?"

"No one's seen him since school let out at three thirty."

The dash on the car taunted them with the current time, which was two hours later.

Dougal swore, then glanced at his sister, who was still hunched over her phone.

"Charlotte's left me about five text messages, asking if I've seen him. I've got three voicemails from her, too. I'm going to—Hang on, I think she's calling me now."

Dougal pushed his speed to the brink of safety, calculating in his mind the distance to Twisted Cedars. Another hour and a half at least.

"Charlotte!" Jamie's voice changed, grew louder and urgent. "I'm with Dou—"

Her explanation was cut off by a torrent of words from the other end of the line. Dougal missed the first few seconds while Jamie turned on the Bluetooth. And then Charlotte's voice came through, clear but frantic.

"—been everywhere! The park, the school, the beach, all his friends! But we just can't find him!"

"Charlotte. Dougal here. Have you called 911?"

"Yes. Wade's at my house right now. I've given him pictures and a video clip of Chester I had on my phone. They've called an Amber Alert. Everyone's looking for him. *Everyone!* So why can't we find him? He had his bike, but how far can a nine-year-old get on a bike? Oh my God, I just can't believe this."

"Is Cory alright?" Jamie's face had turned a pasty white.

"Yes. She's home with me."

"Can you put her on speakerphone?"

Dougal gave his sister's shoulder a quick squeeze. Legally she was still the twins' stepmother. Although that bond would soon be rescinded with the annulment of her marriage to their father, he knew she still cared deeply about the kids.

"J-Jamie?" Cory's voice sounded shattered.

"Honey. Are you okay?"

"Sort of."

"Dougal and I are on our way back to Twisted Cedars right now. We'll be there before seven, I hope. We'll come straight to your house."

"I'm at Aunt Charlotte's."

Jamie glanced at him, her eyes soft with empathy. Moving houses in order to live with their aunt had been one of many adjustment forced upon the twins in the past few months.

"Right. Your aunt Charlotte's place. We'll see you as soon as we can get there. Hang tight, honey. I love you." She ended the call, then drew in a long, shaky breath. "Those poor kids."

Dougal glanced at his sister after she ended the call. "You okay?"

"I suppose…but is Chester? The past few months have been hell for that kid. He hero-worshipped Kyle. Having his father thrown into prison was terrible. And facing the kids at school must be a constant reminder."

"I can imagine." Actually, he didn't need to. He'd been twelve, three years older than Chester, when his father was convicted for killing his second wife and sent to prison. Though Ed had been out of their lives for years, the news had somehow spread through town, and the schoolyard taunts had been brutal.

But the inner shame had proven the more lasting torment.

Jamie drummed her fingers restlessly on her thighs. "I

wouldn't be surprised to find out Chester's run away."

Dougal didn't dare tell her that was a best-case scenario here. His top two fears were first that Chester could have drowned in the ocean or the mighty Rogue River. Or—and this one was just as bad—that somehow Ed Lachlan had gotten his hands on the boy.

"Suppose he did run away," Dougal said. "Where would he go?"

"Somewhere far away. Maybe his grandmother's place in Sacramento?"

Dougal nodded. Kyle's mother had moved there after she divorced her husband, Jim. "That's a long way for a nine-year-old to travel."

"True. Another place he loves is Wolf Creek Camp."

Charlotte had enrolled the kids at the outdoor-living camp for most of the summer, at their request. The wilderness setting had protected them from the media circus that followed the discovery of their mother's body.

"At least that's in the right state. But it's a long car ride to Wolf Creek—I can't see him getting there on a bike. He'd have been picked up by a patrol car for sure if he tried."

"Do you think he'd try the Librarian Cottage?"

The rustic A-frame he was renting from Charlotte had been in the Hammond family for decades. Chester definitely would know how to get there. And the distance—about five miles—was something he could manage relatively quickly on a bike.

Dougal was happy to snatch at this hope, however faint. "Let's check it out on the way to Charlotte's."

chapter three

THE APPROACH TO the Librarian Cottage was down a narrow forestry road, through a tunnel of old-growth cedar forest. Dougal was forced to reduce his speed considerably. "Keep an eye out in case Chester is hiding on the side of the road."

"Believe me, I am."

Dougal glanced at Jamie sharply. Every now and then his sister would say something that reminded him so much of their mother it was painful. The two of them were so similar, they were almost carbon copies. Jamie was kind and empathetic just like their mom. And physically she was similar, too, with her curvy figure, thick dark hair, and deep-set, intense blue eyes.

One of these days Dougal was going to have to find a genetics specialist and ask them to explain how it was possible to create a child who only had one parent's DNA.

For just as Jamie was so like their mom, all his life people had told him he was *just like his dad.*

Did those people realize how it felt, as a kid, to be compared to a man who had beaten his first wife and killed his second? It didn't feel that great as an adult, either.

For a long time Dougal had been happy to escape this

dubious heritage and make his life in New York. But when he'd come back to follow a lead for a new story this spring, he'd decided to stay for two reasons.

One was definitely the local librarian, Charlotte Hammond, who had somehow managed to disarm him completely.

The other was this place.

He stopped in front of the small A-frame, tucked into the forest like a natural part of the landscape. On the front porch were two wicker chairs, which even now invited him to linger.

"I don't see Chester's bike."

"He could have hidden it somewhere." Dougal sprang out of the car and bounded up the path to the front door. He rarely locked the place. Chester could have walked right in.

"Chester? You in here? Don't worry, buddy. No one's upset with you."

The only answer came from his cat, Borden, who jumped off her favorite perch on the back of an armchair and wound her way between his legs.

"Not now, Borden. I've got things to do." Gently he dislodged the cat, who was making the transition from a New York City apartment to a cottage in the middle of a forest rather nervously.

The place was small, it was quick to search, and he was thorough—not just looking under the bed and in both closets but even pulling down the ladder to the attic and making a clean sweep of that as well.

Within ten minutes he was done. After putting Borden

into her travel crate and grabbing a bag packed with her essentials and his, Dougal went outside to deliver the disappointing news. He found Jamie studying the dirt driveway.

"Searching for clues, Sherlock? Want a magnifying glass?"

"Don't mock me. I'm looking for bicycle tracks. I've already checked the old shed. But there are so many great hiding spots in these woods. We'll *never* find him if he's decided to camp out."

"The sheriff's office will have tracking dogs if it comes to that. Come on—let's get going. I'm anxious to talk to Wade and find out what they've done so far."

IT WAS 7:00 p.m. Chester Quinpool had been missing three and a half hours. Sheriff Wade MacKay glanced around Charlotte Hammond's kitchen, noting the slight clutter that children brought to a home—clutter that hadn't been here the last time he visited.

Drawings had been stuck to the refrigerator door as well as a school calendar. Strewn over one side of the island were craft supplies—markers, children's scissors, a stack of construction paper. Under the table was a pair of white sports socks—probably Chester's. A football and a baseball mitt were both on one of the chairs.

This year had already been one of the worst for major crimes in Curry County, even before Chester Quinpool went missing. Wade didn't know how much more his team—or this town—could take.

The trouble had started in the spring when Dougal Lachlan found a body buried in the woods around the Librarian Cottage—a body which was soon identified as being Daisy Hammond, divorced wife of Kyle Quinpool, mother of his twins, and Charlotte's sister.

Then this summer Joelle Carruthers—who turned out to be Dougal and Jamie's half sister—had died in the basement of the library. The earlier drowning of her baby daughter, Josephine, was one crime at least that hadn't occurred in his county.

And now Chester had gone missing.

Wade took the safety of the citizens of Curry County personally. So having a kid go missing on his watch was an affront to everything he believed in.

He was going to find this kid. And bring him home safely.

There was no other option.

"S-sorry, Wade." Charlotte had just finished supplying him with the numbers for Chester's doctor and dentist when it had suddenly occurred to her what these things might be needed for, and she'd burst into tears.

"Take your time."

She was standing with her back to him, at the sink on the pretense of pouring herself a glass of water, which Wade knew she wouldn't drink. So far she'd spurned every offer of tea, coffee, or water that he'd made.

No doubt she felt too nauseous to put anything into her stomach. In her shoes, Wade would probably feel the same. Even though this wasn't her fault, she'd feel like it was. Charlotte was that sort of person.

And Wade knew this because he'd dated her—and had even asked her to marry him.

Thankfully she'd been wise enough to turn him down.

She'd sensed that while he longed for a home, a family, and kids, he hadn't really loved *her*. It had taken Wade some time to figure that out himself.

But while he didn't love Charlotte, he did like her. Very much.

Charlotte was not a woman to draw attention to herself. Her temper was mild, and she would offer her opinion on a matter only when pressed. Despite being pretty, tall, and graceful, she somehow managed to make even her physical appearance understated. A lot had to do with the way she dressed, in the very stereotype of a librarian—in skirts that were too long and baggy blouses and sweaters.

As she swung around to face him, her red-rimmed eyes betrayed her inner anguish. "Do you think someone took him? But who? And why?"

He went to her, offering a friendly, hopefully reassuring hug. "Don't go there, Charlotte. Chances are still good that he went out for a little adventure and lost track of time. Or maybe, given all the pressure he's been under lately, he's run away from home. If that's the case, he can't be far away. We'll find him soon."

"But the dental records…" She shuddered.

"We have to be prepared for the worst, as officers of the law. But you don't. In fact, you should try—"

The side door slammed, and Cory ran into the room. She'd been out on the front porch, waiting for her stepmother, Jamie, and Dougal. Though Jamie and Kyle had only lived together as husband and wife for about a month, it had been long enough for Cory and Jamie to bond.

"They're here!" Cory announced, betraying a heartbreaking faith in the ability of those she loved to magically solve any situation.

Given all the nine-year-old had been through, this naivety struck Wade as particularly poignant. He was afraid Chester's disappearance might have the power to destroy, once and for all, every trace of Cory's childhood faith in adults.

Jamie and Dougal were on Cory's heels. Dougal went straight to Charlotte, enveloping her in a hug that was much more intense than the one Wade had just offered her.

Jamie planted herself in front of him, pushing back her thick hair with both hands. "Any news?"

"We haven't found him yet," Wade hated to admit. "But we've got the entire team working on this, and I've called on the state police as well."

"Has anyone been out to the Librarian Cottage yet?" Dougal asked. "We just swung by on our way. No sign of Chester that we could find, but he knows the place. He could be hiding in the woods. A tracking dog might be a good idea."

Charlotte looked stricken. "I never thought of the cottage. It isn't too far for him to reach on his bike. He could have been there before anyone even started looking for him."

"Good tip," Wade said. "I'll get a team on it right away."

Turning his back on the group, he called one of his top deputies, Frank Dunne. Short, muscular Frank was a bit of a plodder, but he was thorough, and Wade had put him in charge of setting up a command post at the school.

"Sheriff?"

"We need a K-9 unit out at the Librarian Cottage. You'll find clothing items belonging to the missing boy at the station."

"Is this a place Chester has been to before?" Dunne asked.

"Yup. And it's only five miles away. He could have cycled there in the time it took for us to find out he'd gone missing."

"Right. Should I call on Search and Rescue as well? Get a full crew out there?"

"Good idea. Anything turn up at the school so far?"

"Afraid not. We're going door to door, hoping a neighbor might have noticed something. We've talked to all the kids from his class already—and their parents. None of them were aware that Chester had any special after-school plans."

"Well, that's too bad." Finding Chester at a friend's house would have been a best-case conclusion for all concerned.

Wade had just disconnected from the call with Dunne when Tanya Field, his newest deputy, came through the hall with the team who'd been collecting evidence from Chester's room.

Tanya, in her late twenties already showing signs of maturity and level-headedness that gave him great hopes for her future, waved him over. "We found nothing helpful in the bedroom, and all we saw in the family room was a gaming station."

"No sign of the iPad?" Charlotte had explained that her

computer was off-limits to the kids and that they didn't have phones.

"We found the sister's where she said it was. No sign of her brother's."

Wade held up his hand for Tanya to wait, then turned back to the gathering in the kitchen. Charlotte was sitting now with Dougal standing beside her, his hand on her shoulder. Jamie was at the fridge, probably trying to find something to prepare for dinner, while Cory stood next to her, looking lost.

"Charlotte, we can't find Chester's iPad."

"It wasn't in his room? He always leaves it there, usually under his pillow or sometimes in the bathroom, on the counter. Did you check the bathroom?"

"We've looked *everywhere*, ma'am." Tanya nodded. "Unless your house has a secret hiding place somewhere?"

"Not that I know of. And I've lived here all my life."

Cory spoke then, her voice so quiet Wade could hardly hear her. "He took it to school."

"Did you say Chester took his iPad to school, Cory?" Wade repeated to be sure.

"Yes."

"Really?" Charlotte sounded surprised, so Wade inferred Chester wasn't in the habit of disobeying her rules.

To test this theory he asked, "Had Chester done this before? Taken the iPad when he wasn't supposed to?"

Her expression solemn, Cory gave a negative head shake. "This was the first time. And he made me promise not to tell."

Wade and Charlotte had already quizzed Cory on her

brother's disappearance, and she hadn't said a word about the iPad. Wade had to make sure she understood this was no time to put loyalty to her brother ahead of his safety.

"We need to find your brother, so it's important you tell us everything you know. Was there anything else your brother asked you to keep secret today?"

Cory glanced from him to Charlotte and then to Jamie before saying, in the same quiet voice, "No."

Jamie put down the head of lettuce she'd removed from the fridge and then took Cory's hand. "Are you sure, honey? Try to think of anything that was unusual about today. You never know what little thing might help us find your brother."

"Does it have to be today?"

Jamie glanced up at Wade, her eyes quickening with hope, then back at Cory. "It can be anything Chester told you, at any time."

Cory swallowed, then said, "After our first day at school, Chester was really mad. The kids in our class kept calling Dad a jailbird." She ducked her head shyly.

"That was mean." Jamie gave her a hug. "You must have been upset."

"I tried to ignore them. But Chester got mad. That night he told me…he said…"

Cory paused long enough to glance up at her audience. Seeing everyone in the room focused intently on her, she dropped her gaze again, then whispered into Jamie's ear.

Jamie gave her another hug. "You did the right thing to tell me this, honey."

Then Jamie turned to the others. "He told Cory he

wanted to run away."

AT 9:00 P.M. Wade was back at the sheriff's office, setting up the conference room as a central command post for the investigation. So far they'd come up with not a shred of evidence—not one single witness, either—to suggest where Chester had gone after school let out.

Thanks to his sister's sudden forthcoming attitude, they knew there was a high probability the boy was a voluntary runaway, which for many reasons was reassuring. But not totally.

Twisted Cedars was a town locked between the powerful Pacific Ocean on one side and the wilderness of the Cascade Mountains on the other. There were plenty of dangers inherent to both to keep Wade up all night.

Say the boy was hiding in the forest around the Librarian Cottage, for instance. Bears, wolves, cougars...all of those presented dangers. If the boy stayed away from the rivers, he'd risk dehydration. If he didn't, he could unknowingly infect himself with dangerous bacteria that would cause vomiting and diarrhea, which would hasten the process of dehydration.

Or he could be swept away by the current, which in many cases was much more powerful underneath the water than it appeared on the surface.

One wall of the conference room was covered with a huge bulletin board, and on this Wade pinned a photograph of Chester above the map of Curry County. Marnie Philips, his office manager, had already placed pins in the areas where searchers were currently operating.

Carter, Wade's marathon-running deputy, was out with the K-9 unit at the Librarian Cottage. Dunne was still at the school, coordinating volunteers as they swept through the town. Field would remain at the Hammond residence at least until morning. With any luck Chester would sneak home in the wee hours and put this nightmare to rest for all of them.

Wade had called in other off-duty officers to check other potential danger zones. New constructions sites, nearby parks and camping grounds, and the other beaches within reach of a nine-year-old boy on a bicycle.

"Planning to stay here all night?" Marnie placed a to-go cup from the Buttermilk Café on the table. "Largest latte they make. Triple shot."

Wade liked to see himself as a simple man with simple pleasures. As such, his fondness for specialty coffees was something he tried to suppress. But Marnie was onto him. He took a sip, then raised his eyebrows.

"I asked them to add a vanilla shot and whipped cream," Marnie said. "I figured you could use the sugar rush." She perched on the arm of a chair, dangling one of her legs so he couldn't help but notice the purple polish on her sandal-clad toes.

Quickly he glanced away.

Marnie was a force of nature—unstoppable energy, super organized, great at anticipating what needed to be done before he had a chance to ask.

But she was also a distraction in the office. Cute, with a round face and large eyes the color of the Rogue River during spring runoff. Wade often spotted his male staff workers buzzing around her desk, especially forty-year-old Dunne, who had to be at least fifteen years too old for her.

He knew resenting Marnie for her attractiveness was wrong of him. Sexist, politically incorrect, and all of that. But sometimes it *was* hard to concentrate around her.

Not today, however. The issue at hand was simply too big.

"Give me an update," he asked as he took the chair at the head of the table and opened the laptop Marnie had already placed there.

"Here's what I put together for the Amber Alert and our Endangered Missing Advisory." She passed him a sheet of paper describing Chester, his clothing, and his last known location. Also included were several of the photos Charlotte had sent them from her phone, all of which showed a young boy with sandy hair, a snub nose, mouth set in a serious expression, and sad blue eyes.

Wade turned back to the laptop, tapped on his email icon. Earlier he'd asked Jamie to send him any pictures she had of Chester. And she had.

He opened the attachment on her message, then waved for Marnie to take a look. "These predate Chester's father's arrest."

"He looked a lot happier back then," Marnie commented.

"Yeah."

"So what's the theory? You think he's so upset about his dad that he ran away?"

"That's what he told his sister he was planning to do. But

it's also possible he was the victim of an accident...or homicide."

Normally the parents or legal guardians were top suspects when it came to the murder of a child. With Chester's mother dead and his father in prison, that pointed the needle of suspicion directly to Charlotte.

Wade knew he had to remain open to the possibility, even though he personally considered it preposterous.

"And then there's the possibility he was abducted."

"Any suspects there?"

"So far—none. We've checked with the grandfather, who wanted custody of the twins when Kyle went to jail. But we found him drunk and alone in his apartment. And when the state police dropped in on the grandmother in Sacramento they found her alone and befuddled at the idea her grandson was missing."

"So no real suspects for an abduction."

Wade didn't answer. He couldn't help recalling a conversation he'd had with Dougal Lachlan last month. Dougal thought his father, Ed Lachlan, was responsible for killing Joelle Carruthers and her baby daughter. Back then Wade had considered Dougal's theory far-fetched.

But what if it was true?

Could Ed Lachlan still be in Twisted Cedars?

chapter four

AT QUARTER TO midnight Charlotte, Dougal, and Jamie were still on vigil in the Hammonds' kitchen. The crime scene techs had left around ten o'clock, and shortly after that Cory had zonked out on the window seat, along with Borden and the stuffed orca Chester had given her last Christmas.

The twins' bedroom was still off-limits, but even if it hadn't been, Cory wasn't ready to be alone, and Charlotte didn't really want her out of sight anyway.

Several hours ago Stella Ward—the Hammonds' long-time housecleaner, who had worked with Jamie and Dougal's mom, Katie, for many decades—had stopped by with a tuna-noodle casserole. It was half-eaten, congealing on the counter next to the microwave. Charlotte supposed she should put the leftovers in the fridge.

But it seemed too much effort.

Everything seemed too much effort now.

All she could do was stare at her phone, praying for a call, a text, or an email. Every gust of wind from outside had her running to the door.

Please come home.

"This is the worst," Jamie moaned. "I wish there was

something we could *do*. Anyone else want coffee?" Without waiting for an answer she went to make a fresh pot.

Dougal said nothing, just squeezed Charlotte's hand. She knew he'd rather be out in the woods helping in the search, but according to Deputy Field, who would be checking in with them periodically throughout the night, there was no shortage of volunteers, and so Charlotte had asked him to stay here, with her and Cory.

This was her fault. She'd known Chester was troubled, that he was getting taunted at school. If she'd quit her job and homeschooled the twins instead, maybe he would still be here.

"Coffee's ready," Jamie announced presently. "Should I take a cup to Deputy Field?"

"She's outside right now," Dougal said. "She'll probably be back soon."

It should have helped to know that many people were working very hard to find Chester. But it was so late. And there were so many natural hazards in this town. Every minute Chester remained missing, it seemed increasingly likely that something extremely bad had happened to him.

After filling all their mugs with the fresh coffee, Jamie reached for one of the remaining photos on the fridge. It had been taken of the twins at Wolf Creek Camp this summer, and Chester looked...if not happy, at least a little less miserable than normal.

"When I first started dating Kyle, Cory was immediately very friendly and accepting. Chester, not so much."

"He's much more reserved than his sister," Charlotte noted. She'd had the same problem with her nephew when he and Cory had first moved in with her at the end of July.

"The secret with Chester is to tap into his obsession with football." Jamie nudged her brother's chair with her foot. "Thanks to you teaching me how to throw a football when we were kids, I was able to impress Chester with my perfect spiral."

"So you bonded over football? That's rich." Dougal smiled faintly.

"Hey, I was desperate."

"I sympathize. Since Kyle and I didn't exactly get along, I was practically a stranger to the twins when they moved in here. They were so quiet at first—it was awful. Then I decided to show them photographs of their mother growing up, and that was an icebreaker." Remembering what had happened later that evening, Charlotte smiled. "When I tucked them in that night, Chester told me he was too old for a kiss. But after about a half an hour he crept downstairs and said he supposed he wasn't too old for a hug."

"Ah, that's so sweet," Jamie said. "Those poor kids. Kyle going to prison has been so hard on them. And of course they lost their mother when they were so young."

"Thanks to Daisy's postpartum psychosis, I'm not sure they *ever* knew what it was like to have a real mother." Charlotte glanced toward the vacant spot by the sink. Even two years after the car accident that had claimed her parents' lives, it was easy to picture her own mother standing there, always occupied with one task or another but never too busy to pay attention to her children.

She'd been so lucky to be adopted by the Hammonds. Her mother had never made her feel anything but wanted and loved, unlike the older sister for whom she'd been expected to be a playmate.

Mostly Daisy had treated her like a pest, competition for the spotlight that she had so craved. One of Charlotte's deepest regrets was that her sister hadn't lived long enough for them to get over their childhood rivalries and develop a real sisterly bond.

Dougal pushed away from his chair. "I can't sit anymore. I'm going outside to see how Deputy Field is doing."

Charlotte empathized. She was sick of sitting around, too. But Wade had explained that for as long as Chester was missing, she should try to stick close to the house in case he showed up or called the landline.

Charlotte had immediately forwarded the landline to her cell, but she couldn't stand the idea that Chester might make his way home to find the house empty.

So she'd agreed with Wade that she would wait here, for as long as it took.

She'd already called Zoey and explained that the library would remain closed for the time being. For once Zoey hadn't had a word of advice to offer when she heard Chester was missing. She'd actually been quite sympathetic and offered to help with anything Charlotte needed.

But no one could help with what she really needed.

Chester to come home.

Restlessly Charlotte went to the window where Cory was sleeping and gazed into the night. Instead her own reflection stared back at her.

"God damnit!" It killed her to know Chester was out there somewhere and she couldn't help him.

"It's torture, isn't it?" Jamie poured the remains of her coffee into the sink. "I just hope he's okay. That wherever he is, he isn't…"

"Stop. Please." She couldn't stand to hear any of her worst fears put into words.

"Sorry."

"Don't apologize. I know this is just as hard on you." Charlotte left the window and moved to the sink, turning on the hot water and adding a squeeze of dish soap. If she was busy, maybe she could block the terrible worst-case scenarios from popping into her head.

"Do you want me to put the rest of the casserole in a smaller container?" Jamie asked.

"No. Just cover it with foil."

The banal conversation was oddly comforting, and one task seemed to lead to another. Once all the dishes were washed and dried and the counters were spotless, Jamie observed that someone had spilled milk in the fridge. The next thing Charlotte knew, they were emptying the entire contents and washing out the shelves and drawers.

They were considering tackling the freezer next when Dougal came back in. He'd spoken to Deputy Field, and there'd been no developments.

Other than the fact that several news vans had parked across the street, interested in interviewing family members. Deputy Field was at this very moment giving them their marching orders.

Dougal pulled out his phone, then sat at the island and began scrolling. At first Charlotte was puzzled by this—did he really expect to be getting messages at one thirty in the morning?

Then her stomach plunged.

She knew Dougal thought his father had killed Joelle Carruthers and her daughter, Josephine, last July. Did he think Ed Lachlan had taken Chester, too?

"Any emails from LibrarianMomma?" she asked.

Dougal jerked his head up, eyes wide with guilt. "No. Not yet anyway."

She'd been afraid to broach the question earlier. But it wouldn't help to keep sticking her head in the sand. "Could Ed have taken Chester? Do you really think it's possible?"

Jamie clued in then, too. "Come on, Dougal. You'd blame every crime in Curry County on our father if you could."

Dougal's jaw tightened. "It's just a theory."

"Well, it's a crazy theory. No one but you thinks our father—the guy you claim you last saw in New York City as an old man with the assumed name of Monty something-or-other—is now living in Oregon with yet another assumed name and identity."

Cory moaned softly in her sleep, and Jamie paused before continuing in a quieter voice. "Only *you* think this third incarnation of our dad as Brian Greenway managed to track down our half sister, murder her baby, and then force her to hang herself in the basement of our library."

"You're right," Dougal said calmly. "I have no proof Ed was involved in any of that. But I believe he was all the same."

"Okay, on the off chance you're right—why would our father go after Chester? Isn't his next logical target *me*? Isn't that why you dragged me out to the Grassy Knob Wilderness today?"

"I thought so," Dougal agreed. "But if there is one thing Ed Lachlan is not, it's predictable."

Charlotte desperately wished Jamie was right and Ed Lachlan had nothing to do with Chester. She put a hand on Dougal's shoulder. "If Ed is involved, why would he want Chester?"

Dougal's answer was far from comforting.

"For leverage."

AT FOUR IN the morning, Jamie, resigned to the fact that Chester wouldn't be coming home that night, went home to grab a few hours of sleep. Dougal carried a sleeping Cory into the family room and settled her on the shorter of two sofas.

Cory whimpered when he put her down but didn't wake up, not even when Borden jumped up beside her.

Gently Dougal led Charlotte to the second sofa, where he pulled her down and cradled her in his arms. "Try to rest. You'll need your strength tomorrow."

A few minutes later she seemed to be drifting off, but just as her body relaxed, an internal alarm would jerk her awake.

Finally, they both gave up pretending they might sleep and turned on a movie, keeping the volume low.

Cory didn't budge.

"I'm glad she's getting some rest," Charlotte said.

"I wish you would, too."

"How can I?" Charlotte went to the east-facing window, which looked out to the street. Cupping her hands to the glass, she peered out into the blackened world.

"See anything?"

"Those news vans are gone at least." She straightened with a sigh.

"Good," Dougal said, though he supposed if Chester wasn't home by the morning, those vans, and a lot more, would return.

When he spotted Charlotte yawning a few minutes later, he urged her to lie down on the sofa with him again. He held her close, feeling relieved when she finally relaxed. A few minutes later he could tell by her breathing that she was asleep.

As he held his body still so he wouldn't disturb her, his mind raced. He couldn't stop thinking about his father. He wished he had some insight into Ed Lachlan's plan. To Ed, killing a person wasn't a brutal crime—it was a move in a chess game. If Ed had taken Chester, he'd be waiting for Dougal to make the next move.

Dougal had no doubt that Chester's life depended on him making a smart play.

But what should that be?

At some point Dougal finally drifted to sleep himself, awakening at dawn when Charlotte began to stir. Soon after that Cory got up, and they trooped back to the kitchen to go through the motions of having breakfast, even though none of them were hungry.

Deputy Field checked in with them long enough to grab a coffee. Shortly after that the crime scene people returned.

What they hoped to find, Dougal couldn't guess, but according to Wade this was regular procedure.

By eight thirty Dougal was going mad. "I have to do something. This sitting around and waiting is making me insane."

"I feel the same way."

He gave Charlotte a hug, pressing his face against the softness of her hair. Unfortunately she had to stay put, but he just couldn't keep standing guard with her. "I'm going to head to the cabin. I need to get some more clothes for me and a few more tins of food for Borden. At the same time I can check if there's been any progress with the search."

"That would be good." Charlotte moved away from him and put her arm around Cory, who was staring despondently at her bowl of soggy cereal. "But you are going to come back here, right?"

Charlotte rarely asked much of him, and given the current circumstances, it would be churlish of him to deny her. But still he hesitated. He always thought better when he was alone. And he had a hell of a lot of thinking to do right now.

Besides, offering comfort and support during hard times wasn't exactly his strong suit.

"Later tonight," he finally conceded.

He could tell Charlotte was disappointed. But all she did was nod.

GETTING INTO HIS car, Dougal felt both relief and guilt. Charlotte's big gray-clapboard house had begun to feel like a prison. Hopefully this nightmare would end today and they wouldn't have to spend another hellish night like that again.

Though he'd implied to Charlotte he'd be going straight home, Dougal headed for Driftwood Lane and the Buttermilk Café.

He wasn't hungry. But the Librarian Cottage didn't have Wi-Fi or cell-phone coverage, and he needed both.

The café was too cutesy by Dougal's standards—nobody needed to look at a picture of a cute pink pig when they were eating sausages for breakfast—but the coffee was good and the Wi-Fi was free. He settled into a table in the far corner and pulled out his phone.

He found no new messages in his inbox from LibrarianMomma.

But then, he hadn't expected there to be. It was his move, after all.

He took a deep breath, steeling himself. Deliberately seeking contact with Ed Lachlan went against every instinct he possessed.

But Chester's life was in the balance. He had to do this.

First he opened the most recent message he'd sent to his father—a month ago, shortly after Joelle's and Josephine's deaths. He'd been prompted by fear for Jamie's life, certain that the new client she'd gone to meet, Brian Greenway, was really their father—a theory he still believed in.

On that day he'd said, *You win. I'll start the book tomorrow.*

LibrarianMomma's almost instant reply had filled him with revulsion.

That's my boy. I can't wait to begin.

Dougal recoiled from the words again as he reread them. Having that perverted monster refer to him as "my boy" made the bile rise in his throat. Worse, it brought back all his worst insecurities about himself as a person.

Was the darkness that lived in Ed Lachlan also inside Dougal? Perhaps lying dormant, waiting for something to trigger it?

The server came, and he ordered coffee, then waited for her to leave before taking a fortifying breath and then hitting Reply.

Do you have Chester? he typed.

He waited a beat, then pressed Send.

The server returned with his coffee as well as a pitcher of cream. Before he'd taken the first sip, his computer pinged.

LibrarianMomma: *I've been waiting for you to start my book.*

God damnit. The quick answer confirmed he was right—his father had been waiting for him to make the next move.

I'll start today. Just let Chester go.

He leaned back in his chair, almost afraid to blink as he stared at the screen. Again, the response took less than a minute.

I'm calling the shots now, and this is how it's going to work. Here's a link to a chat room. Meet me there in thirty minutes. We'll talk for about an hour, then you go write the first chapter of the book and post it here. I'll read it and give you my comments. And then we'll move on to the next chapter. And so on. Until the book is finished.

Christ! Dougal dug his fingers into his hair, pulling tightly on the roots. Was he serious?

After a moment's consideration Dougal typed: *As soon as Chester is home safe and sound, I'll meet you in the chat room.*

A minute went by. No answer. Dougal sipped the coffee, which dripped into his gut like acid.

Five minutes. Then ten.

Dougal was trying to figure out his next move when a response finally pinged into the account.

You are not setting the terms here.

Damn! he thought.

I need to know Chester is all right.

This time the reply was speedy: *You now have twenty minutes to meet me in that chat room.*

chapter five

DOUGAL WAITED WHILE Wade read the string of email messages between himself and LibrarianMomma. Toe tapping with pent-up anxiety, he raised his gaze to the bookshelves behind the sheriff's desk. This wasn't his first time in Wade's office, but it was his first opportunity to take in the details.

Back when they were in high school, he and Wade had played football together. Fast and rugged, Wade had made a great middle linebacker. With Kyle Quinpool as their quarterback they'd had a lot of success.

But Dougal was relieved to see Wade hadn't put any of those old trophies on display here.

Instead his shelves actually contained books—all related in one way or another to his job. There was a photo of Wade with his father—who had been sheriff himself during the seventies and eighties—with a string of big steelhead trout as evidence of a successful fishing expedition.

The photo was the only personal touch in the entire office. Unless you counted the baseball-sized thunder egg on the corner of his desk. Dougal picked up the rock. It had been sliced in half, exposing the volcanic-ash layers within.

"A gift from my mother."

The words sounded random, until Dougal realized Wade was talking about the rock. He gently replaced it.

"Finished?"

Wade nodded, handing him back the laptop. "What makes you so sure your father has Chester? He didn't make any such claim here."

That was a sticking point, all right. "Because I know how that crazy son of a bitch thinks."

Wade's eyes rolled. Dougal couldn't blame him for being exasperated.

"I suppose I could send your laptop to a computer expert, see if we can trace those emails."

"In theory that's a great idea. In practice, it won't work."

"Why?"

"Back when I started getting these emails about the librarians murdered in the seventies, I asked a guy I know, a real expert in online security. He gave it a try but had to give up. He gave me an explanation—I didn't understand all of it, but somehow Ed has managed to run his messages through a spider web of networks, hijacking other peoples' computers and passing through multiple countries until they finally get lost in what this expert friend of mine calls the dark web. You heard of that?"

"I haven't a clue. Hopefully our experts have, though. If there's a chance Ed Lachlan has Chester, we've got to try."

"Fine." Dougal had already taken the precaution of backing up his laptop, so he relinquished it without further argument. "But I'm going to need something to work on."

Wade stared at him as if he could read the interior workings of Dougal's mind through his eyes. And maybe he could.

"You're going to do what he wants—write the book."

"As long as there's a chance he has Chester, how can I not? Only trouble is the Librarian Cottage doesn't have Wi-Fi. And I can't see talking to the old man at the library or in front of Charlotte."

Wade pondered the situation for a moment. "I'll find you some space here. I can get you a laptop as well. It'll be good to have you close at hand. If you get a lead on Chester's whereabouts we'll want to move quickly."

Dougal hated the idea of working under Wade's thumb. But it made sense. He glanced at his watch. "He's expecting me in the chat room in two minutes. Should we try to record the conversation?"

"Not a bad idea. It would help a lot if we could come up with a shred of evidence supporting the theory that Ed has Chester."

"Yeah. Good luck with that."

They were getting ready to leave the office when the door opened and Marnie Phillips, the round-faced woman with the cute dimples who worked as Wade's assistant or office manager or something, peered in.

"Need anything?"

She obviously had the ability to read minds. Or one man's mind at least.

"Set Dougal up with a private desk and a loaner laptop, will you, Marnie? He'll be working here for a few days."

"The small interview room okay?"

"Perfect. And get Dougal the Wi-Fi code, too."

"Will do. You had some calls while you were busy."

Marnie handed him a stack of notes, then wrote something on a spare yellow Post-it note and beckoned to Dougal. "Follow me."

Marnie led him down a corridor, past a large open area with about six cubicle working stations. She paused to pick up a laptop, then waved a hand indicating all the empty chairs. "Everyone's either out looking for Chester or in the big conference room we're using as a command post." She pointed to an open door about ten feet down the hallway.

Dougal could see people moving around, the sound of several conversations going on at the same time. But then Marnie turned to the right.

The smaller interview room he'd been promised was at the very end of the corridor. Chilly and uninviting. The only window was undoubtedly one-way glass leading to an observation room.

Dougal sat in one of three hard, wooden chairs while Marnie placed his borrowed laptop on the bare table. There was nothing else in the room except a phone. "Cozy."

Marnie gave him an *Aren't you the smart aleck* look, then affixed the Post-it note to the table, right under his nose. The Wi-Fi password, he assumed.

"I'll get you a mug. Coffee is across from the big conference room."

Dougal didn't have time to worry about coffee. He opened the computer and typed in the internet password. As he waited for the connection he noticed Marnie was still in the doorway.

"You worked here long?"

She hesitated. "Two years."

"How long have you had a crush on your boss?"

She glared at him, turned on the heels of her cork-wedged shoes, and left.

Connected, his computer announced.

Dougal found the link to the chat room, registering with the name that had been given to him: DL008. After making sure he was recording, he made his presence known.

DL008: *I'm here.*

LM007: *You're late. Turn on the video.*

Double-oh-seven? Was the old man really channeling James Bond? Talk about delusional.

Dougal took a deep breath. He was about to hurl himself down the rabbit hole. He so did not want to do this. But he clicked the video.

It took a moment for the picture on the computer screen to resolve. And then Dougal was looking at a face most would describe as attractive for a man in his sixties. Ed was now clean-shaven, and Dougal recognized the same strong jaw line and intense eyes he saw in the mirror every morning.

Ed had clipped his hair short, revealing an old scar that traveled from the corner of his eye to his hairline. Other than that, he had no obvious markings suggesting his criminal past.

Dougal stared, searching for traces of the bearded man who had been his neighbor in the apartment in New York. But this man sat erect, no sign of the arthritis that had crippled old Monty. The man's teeth were whiter, his eyes brighter. How had he managed to change all of that?

"Good to see you, son. It's been a long time."

The voice was nothing like the gravely tone he'd assumed

when he'd been Monty. This new version of his father had a pleasant baritone that Dougal remembered from when he'd been a child.

"You look different."

Ed laughed. "You don't. It's like watching old video footage of me, back when I was your age."

Just like your father. Dougal had heard the phrase a lot when he was growing up. People used it to describe his looks, his sullen behavior, even his prowess on the football field. No matter why people said the words though—whether they meant them as a compliment or pejoratively—hearing them always made Dougal's skin crawl.

"Let me see Chester."

The smile on Ed Lachlan's face faded, and he shook his head. "I'm not playing games with you, son. Not this time. A month ago you promised you were going to write my story. So far you haven't delivered a single word."

"I'll do it this time. We just need to know Chester's all right."

"I'm not interested in harming that boy. I just want my son to tell the world my story."

Damn it, the old man was being too clever by half. Not admitting to kidnapping Chester, but not denying it, either. He had Dougal on the ropes, though, since the possible price was too high to risk.

"Where do you want to start? Your childhood?" Earlier that summer Dougal had tracked down Ed's adopted sister, who'd told him all about the abuse Ed had suffered at the hands of their adopted parents. Dougal had assumed Ed would want to go into this phase of his life in detail.

But as usual, Ed surprised him.

"Screw that. Let's begin when it gets interesting. 1972, and I've just turned twenty-two. Do you know what happened then?"

"You found your adoption papers and then broke into the agency that had brokered your adoption to find the name of your birth mother."

"Smart boy." Ed beamed with a combination of amusement and pride. "It didn't take me long to find out where Shirley Hammond lived. And of course, once I knew that, I had to pay her a visit."

May 15, 1972, Librarian Cottage outside of Twisted Cedars, Oregon

NOT MUCH SCARED *Shirley Hammond anymore, but when she heard the knock on her door shortly after sunset on a Friday evening in May, she felt a premonition of dread. Her brother and his wife, normally her only unexpected visitors, were on their annual vacation in California.*

No one else would dream of visiting her without making plans ahead.

She grabbed the rifle she kept under her bed and made sure it was loaded.

Her younger brother, John, didn't like her living in this cottage in the woods, so many miles from civilization. But Shirley wasn't afraid of bears, wolves, or cougars. And she didn't mind the isolation. Fact was she never felt alone.

Her best friends were in books. Hercule Poirot had spent

many an evening chatting amiably with her on her worn chintz couch. Other days Miss Marple would pop over for a spot of tea, or Tuppence and Tommy would appear, hot on the chase of a new unsolved murder.

Shirley read other authors beside Agatha Christie, of course. As a librarian she felt it was essential to be grounded in the classics and aware of the hottest bestsellers as well.

But those were the books she'd studied in college and read during her lunch hours at work. When she was here, at her home, her sanctuary, she preferred her mysteries.

The second knock came, louder than the first.

"Who's there?"

"Why don't you open the door and see?"

The taunting tone was infuriating. Did this goon really think he could frighten her? Shirley hoisted the rifle to her shoulder and then angled her body so she could release the dead bolt. "Hands where I can see them, or I'll shoot."

The door swung inward. Cast in the rosy glow of twilight was a young man in his early twenties—handsome, with dark hair, broad shoulders, and an uneasy grin. He was holding out his hands palms upward, as if seeking a handout.

She was positive she'd never seen him before, but there was something familiar about him all the same and it frightened her. She tightened her hold on the gun. "Whatever you want, I don't have it. I suggest you go back where you came from. I'm an excellent shot."

"But I went through so much to find you...Mother."

If she had a weak heart, it would have stopped right then. But Shirley's heart was strong. And so was she. "I'm no one's mother."

"You sure haven't acted like one. But you gave birth to me,

all right. On this very day, twenty-two years ago."

She'd noted the date when she woke up, of course. She always tried not to, prayed for the year when May fifteenth would be a day like any other.

"I want you to leave. Right now." While keeping him in her sights, she pushed the door with her knee. But he moved fast, inserting his body into the gap, forcing her to jump backward in order to keep her rifle pointed at his chest.

"Get out, I said!"

"Or what? Are you going to shoot me?"

Years later, Shirley Hammond would remember this moment and the mocking grin on his face. She'd wish desperately she could turn back the clock. But on that May evening she didn't shoot him. She let him stay.

chapter six

DOUGAL'S FINGERS TREMBLED as he pressed Enter, effectively sending the first installment of the book to LibrarianMomma. Repulsed to the point of nausea, he gripped the sides of his chair and took a few deep breaths.

Listening to his old man recount his first meeting with his birth mother had been excruciating. Dougal had attempted to tune out his emotions, to act the part of a courtroom stenographer and focus on the words as combinations of letters rather than their abstract meanings.

But it was hard, knowing Ed was talking about Charlotte's adopted aunt, not to mention Dougal's biological grandmother.

Ed made Shirley Hammond sound tough as nails, whereas up until now Dougal had imagined she would have Charlotte's calm, gentle personality.

Since Charlotte had been adopted, though, it had been irrational for him to project the older woman's personality on the other.

Ed had started their session with his "vision" for the book. He wanted most of the scenes written from his point of view, with a few scenes from Shirley's vantage point thrown in as counterpoint.

It was an approach Dougal himself had used in his previous books, contrasting the perpetrator and the victim to maximize the drama. So he hadn't protested the idea.

Their chat had gone on for over an hour, at which point Ed instructed Dougal to disconnect and write the first chapter.

Dougal had done so, not worrying about style, pacing, or word choice. He'd just dumped out the words, basically as the old man had fed them to him. Two scenes in Ed's point of view and one in Shirley's.

Dougal suspected his father had the entire story already plotted in his head, probably he could have authored it himself. Only what would be the fun in that? This way he got to torment his famous author son in the process. No doubt he fantasized about both of their names on the book cover—creating the illusion of a father-son relationship—the two of them making the *NY Times* best-selling list and appearing on talk shows together.

No chance of that happening, of course. Ed was going to end up back in prison, one way or another. If not for the murders that were going to be the focus of this book, then for the murders of Joelle and her daughter—and kidnapping Chester.

A knock sounded on the closed door, and then Wade entered. "How did it go?"

"Brutal." Dougal didn't need to say more. Wade knew how he felt about his father. "But the first chapter is done. I just emailed it to him. I'm guessing it won't take him long to read it and be back to me with comments. Thought I'd run home to grab a shower and shave while I have the chance."

"That's a good idea. By the way, Marnie's made arrangements to have your laptop examined by one of the FBI's computer experts. I know it's a long shot, but we have to try and trace those emails."

"Speaking of Marnie...how old is she? She looks about twenty, but I suspect she's the kind of woman who looks younger than her true age."

Wade's eyes narrowed. "Why do you ask?"

"Just wondering if I should encourage her crush on you. Or suggest she look elsewhere."

Damn, it was cute seeing the sheriff blush.

"I'd rather you focused on the job at hand."

Dougal's sense of fun vanished. "Don't worry about me. I want Chester home and Ed back behind bars more than you do."

"Good to hear. While you're home you better pack your toothbrush and a change of clothes. We'll want to keep the lines of communication between you and Ed open as much as possible. If he wants to chat all night—I want you to be here for him."

"Yeah." Dougal had to agree, even though it would mean breaking his promise to Charlotte.

"With staff working around the clock there'll be lots of sandwiches and other snacks on hand. Feel free to help yourself."

As Dougal followed Wade down the corridor, he paused to glance inside the room being used to manage the investigation. The long wall was covered with maps, lists, names, and photos. Every inch of the large rectangular table held computer equipment, files, and stacks of paper.

"Any progress?"

"We're figuring out lots of places Chester *isn't*, if you call that progress." Wade rubbed his jaw, worried. "I know you figure Ed has the boy. But there's still a chance the kid is hiding out somewhere."

"Have you still got guys searching the woods around my place?"

"Yeah. The K-9 unit is out there with about thirty volunteers from Search and Rescue. Unless we find something—a bike tire print, a scrap of fabric, anything like that—we'll be pulling out at the end of the day."

"Okay." Dougal put a hand on Wade's shoulder. "You look as beat as I feel."

"Not going to be much rest for any of us until we find him."

Dougal nodded. He and his old friend had had their differences. But they were definitely on the same side now.

ON THE DRIVE to the Librarian Cottage, Dougal couldn't help thinking about the first message he'd received from his father, back in May of this year. At the time he'd had no idea "LibrarianMomma" was his old man.

His father had been crafty. Since Dougal had refused to take his calls or open his emails, Ed had snared him by using the moniker of LibrarianMomma and dangling a series of unsolved mysteries under his nose. As a true-crime writer looking for a subject for a new book, Dougal hadn't been able to resist.

If he'd just ignored the bait, Joelle Carruthers and her baby daughter might still be alive. Chester would be in his classroom right now—bored, probably, but at least safe.

On his drive out of town Dougal placed a call to Charlotte, filling her in on the latest developments and promising to drop by later that evening, warning her he wouldn't be able to stay long.

"That's okay. I appreciate what you're doing. I know you don't want to write your father's story."

"If it helps Chester, it'll be worth it. How's Cory doing?"

"I decided to send her to school. It's the best thing for her. Hanging around here is soul-sucking."

"Hopefully it won't be for much longer." But he was afraid Ed Lachlan wouldn't let the boy go until the entire book was written. And even then—well, Dougal didn't feel the odds were in their favor.

Unless…maybe the old man was taking advantage of the boy's disappearance to coerce Dougal into writing the book. There was always that possibility. Dougal allowed himself to hope. Maybe, right this moment, a bloodhound was on Chester's trail. Any minute now a volunteer might be radioing in the happy news: *We've found him!*

But as soon as he rounded the last corner to the cottage, Dougal's faint hope died. Over a dozen vehicles were jammed around the property. The only people in view were two volunteers manning a makeshift table on the porch.

From their expressions it was instantly clear that no good news was forthcoming.

Dougal paused, imagining the cottage as it must have appeared to a twenty-two-year-old Edward Lachlan back in

May of 1972. The structure itself hadn't changed since then.

What had Ed's intentions been in that fatal moment before he met his birth mother?

Had he expected her to welcome him with open arms? And would things have ended differently if she had?

Shaking off his introspections, Dougal identified himself to the volunteers, who, grim-faced, confirmed the lack of progress in locating Chester or any clues to his whereabouts.

Inside, Dougal found Deputy Duane Carter, thin, with a taut, muscular, runner's body, writing reports at the kitchen table. According to Charlotte, who devoured the local paper religiously each Wednesday, Duane had placed third in his age group in the Dog Days of August Marathon two weeks ago.

Three cheers for Duane.

"So. How's it going?"

Duane glanced up at him. "No sign of Chester, or his bike, yet. But we're going to keep looking until sunfall."

"I won't get in your way. Just need a shower and to pack a few things."

Fifteen minutes later Dougal was out the door. As he walked toward his vehicle he was remembering the last time Chester had been at the cottage, less than two weeks ago. Dougal had invited Charlotte and the twins for an end-of-the-summer barbeque the night before the first day of school.

Cory had been a chatterbox, telling them all about her experiences at Wolf Creek Camp. Both the twins seemed to love the place, though Chester, as per usual, hadn't talked about it much.

The only time Dougal had seen Chester's face light up

was when he asked Dougal about his experiences playing high school football with his dad. He clearly had his father on a pedestal, and Dougal, though not normally one to sugarcoat the truth, had taken pains to make Kyle out to be the hero in every story.

The truth was Kyle had been a talented quarterback, but he would have been even better if he hadn't tried to make himself the star of every play.

But that was Kyle. The golden-haired, blue-eyed charmer was used to having life go his way. Dougal had always expected this character flaw would eventually land him in trouble. But he'd never guessed his old football buddy would go so far as to bury his wife's body in order to escape retribution for what had, in all likelihood, been an accidental death.

On the day of the barbecue, Dougal had wondered if the twins would ask about the spot where he'd found their mother's body. They hadn't. But when they were ready, he would show them. Hopefully the Shasta daisies he'd planted there would still be blooming.

CHARLOTTE HAD THOUGHT cleaning out her closet would help make the time pass more quickly, but she couldn't focus on even this simple task for more than five minutes at a time. The twins' bedroom across the hallway kept drawing her.

The crime scene techs had finished with the room, but she was loath to clean up the residue of fingerprint powder. She found she wanted to touch nothing but just stand in the doorway and run through the memories she had of Chester.

The kids had been under her care for less than two months—and at least three weeks of that time they'd spent at summer camp. Yet already they felt like *hers*. Their imprint on this room was unmistakable. She'd given them permission to put three posters each on the wall. Chester's were all from the 49ers, of course. His father had taken him to a game once, and he still talked about the experience.

Where is he now? Is he okay? Will he ever get to go to another football game?

With each question, another layer of pain seemed to weigh down her heart. Charlotte pressed her knuckles into her teeth, welcoming the distraction of physical pain over mental.

It wasn't even four o'clock. She didn't know how much more of this she could take. She wished someone would phone—if not with good news, then with a tidbit of something positive. Surely a nine-year-old boy could not disappear without a trace.

And then, as if she had conjured it, the doorbell rang. And immediately hope and fear rose equally within her until she remembered the time. This would be Cory. Her best friend's mother had offered to drive her home from school.

Charlotte raced down the stairs and flung open the door, suddenly anxious to make sure that Cory, at least, remained unharmed.

And of course she was. Her niece, with her small heart-shaped face so like her mother's, looked at her with questioning eyes.

"No news on your brother, I'm afraid." Charlotte pulled the girl in for a hug, then glanced up at Bailey Landax. It was hard not to resent the other woman's well-groomed state when she herself looked like hell.

But then Bailey was a Realtor. Looking attractive and professional was important to her success. With the closing of Quinpool Realty, business must've been booming. Even Jamie had purchased her new home from Bailey.

"How are you doing, Charlotte?"

"Is Chester home yet?" asked her daughter, Paige.

"No." Charlotte shook her head grimly. "I'm afraid not."

"I'm sorry to hear that."

Bailey put a hand on Charlotte's shoulder. She probably meant the touch to convey sympathy, but for some reason this woman had always struck a false note with Charlotte.

Still, Charlotte knew Cory really enjoyed Paige's company, so she was glad to hear Bailey say, "I'll be glad to drive Cory to and from school tomorrow as well, if—well, if you would like me to."

In other words, if Chester was still missing.

"Thank you," Charlotte said, barely managing to get out the words without crying.

"Oh, absolutely." Bailey hesitated, then took a step forward and lowered her voice. "I did hear Cory talking about something with Paige. I thought it might be important, and so I suggested she tell you."

"Is it to do with Chester?"

"Yes, it is. Go on, Cory, tell your aunt the same thing you told Paige."

Worried lines appeared on Cory's forehead as she glanced from Bailey to Charlotte.

Charlotte gave her niece's hand a squeeze. "It's okay,

honey. Take your time."

Cory swallowed. "W-well, it was after school a few days ago. We were walking home when the football coach told Chester he wanted to talk to him."

Charlotte was confused. The school the twins went to had a gym teacher but not a football coach per se. "Were you still on the school grounds?"

"Not anymore. We were walking past the pink house, the one with the bird houses."

Charlotte nodded. "I know exactly the place you're talking about. So this football coach—was he someone you knew?"

"No."

"Are you saying a strange man just walked up to your brother and started talking to him?"

"I-I guess. But he looked like a coach—he had a ball cap and a whistle on a rope around his neck. He wanted to know if Chester was planning to play football when he was older. He said Chester looked like someone who would be a natural."

Charlotte put out a hand to the doorframe, feeling suddenly unsteady. She took a deep breath, then nodded at Bailey. "Thank you for bringing this to my attention. We need to let the sheriff know right away."

"Of course. I think driving by the house was what made Cory remember. I hope it helps."

Charlotte thought she said thank-you again before closing the door, but she wasn't sure. She was too focused on Cory, trying to read from her expression if she realized how important her story might be.

"Come and sit down," she told her niece. "I'm really glad you remembered this detail. It could be important, so I'm going to phone Sheriff MacKay, all right?"

"Okay," Cory said softly.

Charlotte kept a reassuring hand on Cory's back as she made the call. Her eyes fell on the butter she'd removed from the fridge earlier, planning to make cookies with her niece once she was home.

Was she deluding herself to hope that this clue might be the key? That before the cookies were ready, her nephew might be home?

chapter seven

AFTER BEING ADMITTED into the inner sanctum of the sheriff's department, Dougal was heading toward his room at the far back of the building when he almost collided with Wade. Wade had his hat in one hand, SUV keys in the other.

"Dougal." Wade looked pressed, but he paused to talk. "Charlotte just called. Apparently Cory noticed Chester talking to the high school football coach on the way home from school one day—she thinks it was on Monday."

Dougal knew Brad Scott. He'd been a senior when Dougal, Kyle, and Wade were juniors. He'd played four years of college football, on the same scholarship that had later been offered to—and refused by—Kyle.

"Where did this happen?"

"Cory says Scott approached Chester during their walk home from school."

"I suppose Brad could have been asking about Kyle."

"Cory said they were talking about football. The coach was buttering up Chester, saying he thought he looked like a kid with potential."

"You're right. There's something off about it."

"I'm going to talk to Scott now. Field is getting a statement from Cory and Charlotte." Wade's eyes narrowed. "You going another round with the old man?"

Dougal held up his phone, which had chimed with new email messages about five times on his drive back to town. "I've been summoned."

"Did he like the first chapter?"

"God help me, he did."

"It's a video chat?"

"Yes. A different chat room than the last time."

"Can you tell where he's contacting you from? Anything in the background that might be a clue?"

"Afraid not. He's strung up something on the wall behind him. Looks like a white bedsheet."

"Not much to go on there. Keep me posted if anything else comes up."

"Will do."

Dougal carried on down the hall, pausing to grab a slice of pizza from the big conference room. Only Marnie was in there at the moment, logging information into one of the computers. She paused briefly but when she saw it was him immediately lowered her gaze and resumed typing.

The telltale red stain on her cheeks gave her away, though.

She *did* have a crush on her boss. Dougal wondered if Wade had guessed. Knowing him, probably not. Wade was pretty astute when it came to running the sheriff's department. But when it came to romance—especially his own—he didn't have a clue.

His replacement laptop was waiting on the table, just as he'd left it. Dougal opened the machine and, while he waited for it to warm up, devoured his pizza. He might as well build up his strength now because for sure once he started chatting with the old man again, his appetite would be gone.

As he ate, Dougal reread the email he'd skimmed earlier on his phone. LibrarianMomma sounded so excited, it was nauseating.

Yeah! That's perfect. You're off to a good start. I'm ready to work on the next chapter as soon as you are.

Christ, he thought. *The sick pervert was totally getting off on this.*

Dougal took a deep breath, then followed the link and signed into the new chat room. He couldn't help but flinch when his father's face almost immediately filled the computer screen.

"You got to admit, son. Makes a damn good story, doesn't it?"

Dougal swallowed down his disgust at the word "son." Though he didn't remember much about his old man, he knew that if he asked him not to call him that, he'd do it more.

"Want to pick up where we left off?"

"That's the idea."

"What's Chester doing while we work on this?" Dougal slipped the question in but wasn't surprised when all Ed Lachlan did was scowl and shake his head.

And then he started talking.

"For as long as I could remember, I'd dreamed about finding my mother, even though I knew she never wanted me. What a fool I was to think she'd be happy to see me now..."

EXPOSED

May 15, 1972, Librarian Cottage outside of Twisted Cedars, Oregon

"WHY ARE YOU here?" Shirley kept hold of the rifle, even though she already knew the moment to use it had passed...

"Why, to introduce myself. Don't you think it's time we met? I'm Edward Lachlan, but I've always wondered...if you'd kept me, what would you have named me?"

He was playing games with her, like a cat toying with a mouse. But she was older than him. Smarter, too. She had to convince him he couldn't get to her. "I was a mere teenager when all that happened. There was never any question of me naming, or keeping, you."

"Really?"

Edward turned his back to her, and before she realized what he was doing, he'd pulled up his T-shirt to reveal skin so red and scarred it seemed reptilian.

For just a moment Shirley felt the urge to reach out and touch the raised, angry-looking welts. Instead she curled her fingers into her palms. "I didn't have anything to do with that."

"Not even a sympathetic word from my own mother? Especially considering it was you who gave me—an innocent infant—to the monsters who did this?"

"Stop!" Shirley Hammond covered her ears. "I don't want to hear any more about how they treated you. I was just a kid myself."

"You don't want to hear about the beatings?" He circled her, forcing her to twirl in place in order to keep her eyes on him.

"But I came such a long way to tell you my story, Mother.

Maybe, instead, I should tell you about the way they starved me, made me scrounge and steal for enough food to stay alive. Or perhaps you'd like to hear how they treated my younger sister like a princess—just to make sure I knew that it was me, *not* them, *who was the problem."*

She closed her heart to his words. It was a skill she'd taught herself long ago. He was just a character in a novel. This was merely a story, and she could choose to stop reading whenever she wished.

With a calm voice she pointed out, "None of that was my fault."

"But you're the one who gave me to them."

Suddenly it was not a man with a mocking tone in front of her but a sad little boy, asking why she'd abandoned him. The old pain slammed into her then, and she was shocked that after all these years it could still hurt so much.

She wouldn't go back there. She couldn't. Shirley pushed back against the darkness, imagined shoving it between the covers of a book and replacing it on the furthest, darkest corner of a bookshelf.

"My parents made the arrangements."

"But they're dead now."

Yes. He'd done his homework. Her parents had both died prematurely—her father from a heart attack and her mother from a bad fall down the basement stairs. And she was glad of it. She had never stopped blaming them. The legacy, it seemed, was to be continued.

She set the rifle on the kitchen table. "Fine. If you need someone to blame, then let it be me."

The man, the stranger, her son, stared back at her.

What was he looking for from her, if not guilt? "Would it

make you feel better to beat me the way they used to beat you?"

She stood before him, an easy target, but he remained motionless.

She turned her gaze to the gun. "Or maybe you'd rather shoot me."

The terror she expected to feel was absent. This was the price you paid when you locked away some of your emotions. Eventually it became harder and harder to feel anything at all.

She watched his face, saw him study the gun as if considering her suggestion. But then he swallowed and shook his head.

"When I was a boy I used to dream you would come and save me."

Shirley blocked out the image his words painted. No one had saved her, either. "You survived without me."

"Only because I was waiting for this day. I'm going to make you pay." He put his hand on the gun. "But not with this."

He left then, and Shirley was relieved. It wasn't until a few days later that she noticed one of her red scarves—it had been draped over the back of the sofa, along with the cardigan she'd worn to work that day—was missing. At the time it didn't seem a matter of much consequence.

chapter eight

WADE PARKED HIS SUV across the street from the high school, alongside an overgrown hedge but with a clear view of the football field. A practice was in session, and Coach Brad Scott stood out as not only the oldest man present but also the largest. The impressive bulk Scott had sported during his years as defensive end with the Broncos had gone to fat, and even distributed over his six-foot-plus frame he looked obese.

It didn't seem that long ago that Wade and his friends had been playing football on this same field. Wade counted back. Sixteen years. Hell, that number made him feel old.

In Wade's memory, practices back then had been tests of will, skill, and physical stamina. But the guys on the field today seemed to be making a lackluster effort, while Coach Scott was spending more time watching his phone than his players.

Shortly before half past five, Scott waved the guys off the field. Wade got out of his vehicle and made his way slowly across the street. He paused before approaching Scott, just in case he had last-minute questions to answer, but it seemed the team couldn't get off the field fast enough.

"So they can run after all."

From Scott's startled expression, he obviously hadn't noticed Wade before now. The coach glanced from him to the departing players.

"The season isn't shaping up to be one of our best." He tucked his phone into his jacket pocket. "Can I help you, Sheriff?"

Up close, Coach Scott was looking rough. His eyes were bloodshot and his gray-speckled goatee was on its way to becoming a full-on beard.

"I hope so. You may have heard a local boy, nine-year-old Chester Quinpool, has gone missing." Wade pulled out a photo.

Scott gave it a brief glance. "Yeah. That's tough. Hope you find him soon."

The words were right, but the man displayed no real emotion. Wade would have expected more from a man who coached young men and even had two sons himself.

"It's been more than twenty-four hours, so we're pretty concerned. Have you seen Chester recently?"

"Why would I?" With a spiritless shuffle, reminiscent of the young men he was supposedly training, Scott made his way to the bleachers lining the west side of the field.

Wade followed. "Well, the kid is a huge football fan."

"I haven't noticed him hanging out at any of our practices, if that's what you mean."

"Have you seen him anywhere else? Maybe around the grade school?"

"No. Like I said, why would I? I'm a high school coach, not a grade school babysitter." Scott picked up a clipboard that had been resting on the lower rung of the bleachers.

"Maybe so. But we have a witness who says you stopped Chester on his way home from school a few days ago. Monday afternoon, shortly after three thirty. This witness says you were asking Chester if he had plans to play football when he was older."

Scott let out a sound more like a bark than a laugh. "My boys might be pussies this year. But I haven't stooped to recruiting nine-year-olds."

"So you deny talking to him?"

Suddenly Scott went still. He turned slowly until his gaze was locked with Wade's. "I've never spoken to Kyle Quinpool's boy in my life. Except maybe a time or two in Boy Scouts, but that was last year."

"So you know who he is?"

"Of course I do. It's a small town. Kyle sold my wife and me our first home. Daisy and my Sharleen used to be friends. She was something, that Daisy, huh? Sharleen had the body, but Daisy had the face of an angel."

Wade studied his eyes. This man was talking too much. He sounded nervous, like he was hiding something.

"How old are your sons?"

"Jason's eight. Brock's eleven."

"Where are they right now?"

"Home with their mother, far as I know."

Wade remembered Sharleen well. They'd been in the same class at school. As she'd matured Sharleen had spent more time hanging out with older kids, including Brad Scott—and also, Wade remembered suddenly, Daisy Hammond.

He wondered how she had taken the recent news of Daisy's death and illegal burial.

"Okay. Well, I guess I'll head to your home next and see if Sharleen has anything to add."

"Go ahead and talk to her." There was a bitter tinge to Scott's words now. "I'm sure she'd love to get in her two cents."

Since there was no vehicle nearby and Scott seemed about to start walking, Wade offered him a lift. "We're headed the same way."

"Actually, we're not. Sharleen and I split up this summer."

Scott lowered his head, but not before Wade saw the gleam of sudden tears.

Was this why the coach seemed so out of sorts?

"She kicked me out in August. We still share one vehicle, and since she had to take our eldest for a doctor's appointment today, she got it. That's why I'm on foot," he added, unnecessarily.

"Sorry to hear that, Brad."

"Yeah, well, I'm not the man she married, right? Once I was a super athlete, pulling in six figures. Now I'm just an overweight high school coach who drinks too much. Never mind that she was the one who wanted to move back to Twisted after my pro career ended. I could have taught college at least."

Wade put a hand on the other man's shoulder. They were about the same height, but Scott had at least sixty pounds on him. "Let me give you a lift home at least."

The coach shrugged. "I guess."

The address Wade was given was only six blocks away,

long enough for Scott to let him know Sharleen thought he was too hard on their boys.

"A man needs to teach his kids how to throw a football, right? According to Sharleen, my corrections were hurtful to their self-esteem. Can you imagine that? How the hell do you teach a boy to throw a god damned spiral if you're only allowed to tell him what a good job he's doing?"

Wade didn't answer. He was thinking of the times he and his father had tossed a football around in their backyard. His dad hadn't been much of a talker. He'd shown Wade what to do, and Wade had done his best to imitate. Eventually he'd gotten it right.

At some point Wade hoped to do the same with his own kids.

Of course, he'd have to find a wife first.

"Here we are." He parked outside of the weather-beaten clapboard house, taking note of the side entrance to the basement suite.

"Thanks for the lift, Sheriff. Hope you find the Quinpool boy. That family sure has had its share of hard times."

"That it has." Wade got out of the driver's seat, following Brad Scott as he made his way toward his humble new home.

Scott paused once they reached the property line. "Well. See you around."

Wade stood his ground. "I'll see you to the door, if you don't mind."

"What the hell? You want to check out my place? You actually think I've got the kid—that I'm some sort of pervert?"

"No, Scott, of course not. I figured since I'm here I might as well check the backyard. A small boy like Chester could be hiding anywhere. If it was your kid," he concluded, "you'd want me to cover all the bases, wouldn't you?"

"I suppose." Scott sounded somewhat mollified as he dug out his keys.

Wade made a show of examining the yard and peering over fences into the adjacent properties. When Scott opened his door, he was able to get a good look over the man's shoulder.

There was no sign of anything amiss, unless you counted the presence of a half-empty bottle of bourbon on the kitchen table.

"I'm a fan of Jim Beam myself," he commented, untruthfully.

"Is that a hint? I thought law men weren't supposed to drink on the job."

"I've been working overtime for about twelve hours now. I guess I'm entitled."

"Sounds fair to me." Scott headed inside, obviously expecting Wade to follow, which he did.

While Scott pulled two glasses from the cupboard, Wade had a good look around. The bachelor apartment was a big open space with a bed in one corner, a sofa and TV in the other, and the kitchen tucked up close by the door.

There were two doors off the kitchen, both of them open. One led to a bathroom, the other to a dark space with no windows.

Once he had his bourbon in hand, Wade moved closer to the second door. Inside was a hot water heater and electrical panel. If Scott had abducted Chester, he sure as hell wasn't hiding him here. Of course, Scott could have Chester hidden someplace out of town. But having to share a vehicle with his estranged wife would make that problematic.

"Nice place. It's small, but you've got everything you need."

"You're being polite, Sheriff. It's a shithole."

Wade made quick work of the bourbon, then claimed he needed to get back to work, which he did. On the way to his vehicle, he noticed a pink house across the street. The very house that Cory had mentioned when she described the meeting between her brother and the coach.

A woman in her seventies answered the door when he knocked. She was small boned and frail looking, and her voice, when she spoke, was very soft.

"Hello, Sheriff. Are you here to ask about the missing boy again?"

"Yes." He introduced himself and took note of her name. "I take it one of my people has already questioned you?"

"Oh, yes. Two of them, in fact. But I'm afraid I wasn't able to help. I wasn't out in my garden at all on Wednesday, so I didn't see the children that day. Sometimes I do, you see. But not on Wednesday."

"What about on Monday? Did you happen to notice Chester talking to a man?"

"Not Monday, no. But I was cutting back my roses on Tuesday, and I did see the children then. No man. No adults at all, just the usual pack of Thompson children as well as the Quinpool twins."

"They always walk home together?"

"Usually. But on that day Chester was running ahead of the rest..." She paused thoughtfully. "I'm afraid a couple of the Thompson boys were teasing him about his father. That is, I did hear the term 'jailbird.' Not very nice, if you ask me."

"No. Not nice at all. Thank you, Mrs. Stockman. I appreciate your help."

A DELICIOUS AROMA—WADE'S first guess was beef chili—wafted from the open windows of Coach Scott's family's home, along with the sounds of someone cooking and a TV playing in the background.

Sharleen opened the door almost immediately after he knocked. "Sheriff MacKay. I saw your vehicle pull up in front of our house. Is everything okay?"

Sharleen was wearing calf-length leggings, a red sports bra, and a sleeveless white top scooped low at the front. In high school she had possessed the sort of body that made men—even those who knew better—stop and stare. Unlike her husband, who had packed on the pounds in the intervening years, Sharleen seemed to have worked hers off. Now she had the slender, muscular build of a woman who worked out religiously.

"Just making a routine call. We're canvasing the area to see if anyone has seen Chester Quinpool in the past two days." Wade pulled out the photo, but Sharleen waved it away.

"You don't need to show me that. I know Chester very

well. He and Jason were in Boy Scouts together last year. Jason hated Boy Scouts—only went because his father made him."

She paused as the sound of an argument erupted from a nearby room. "You boys be quiet. We've got the sheriff visiting."

Immediately the ruckus ended.

Wade focused back on Sharleen. "I take it you haven't seen him?"

"No. I was out searching this afternoon with a bunch of the other parents while my boys were in school. I take it there's been no news since then?"

"Afraid not."

"That's so sad. I can't believe the trouble that poor family has had. I'm still not over the shock of finding out his mother is dead. I mean, I guess I knew it was a possibility, maybe even a probability. But until you find out for sure, you can't help but hope."

"You and Daisy were good friends in high school, weren't you?"

"When we were younger. By high school, I was hanging out with an older crowd." She paused, sighed. "Dating Brad Scott wasn't the smartest thing I ever did. But hey, I was young and stupid."

"I was just talking to Brad, and he told me the two of you are separated. He seems pretty upset about it."

"Sure he's upset. He had it good here. I cooked, cleaned, and looked after his kids so he could watch football and drink beer all weekend."

She made no effort to hide the bitterness in her voice,

and Wade wondered if Scott was guilty of more than just watching football and drinking beer.

"As far as you know, did Brad ever have anything to do with Chester? Maybe back when the boys were in Boy Scouts together?"

Sharleen pulled back. "Brad and Chester? What are you implying, Sheriff?"

"These are just routine questions."

She narrowed her eyes. "Brad may not be father- or husband-of-the-year material. But he's no kidnapper."

"I never—"

"I think you'd better go, Sheriff. I've got to get dinner on the table for my boys."

chapter nine

"SEAN SAYS THIS is on the house." Mia O'Brian placed two heaped plates containing the Linger Burger and Twisted Fries Special on the table in front of Wade.

"Thanks, Mia. Hopefully I don't have to eat all this myself." Fifteen minutes ago Wade had left a message for Dougal to meet him at the local pub. He thought it would do his old friend good to get out of the office, take a bit of a breather.

Truth be told, he needed the break, too.

"If he doesn't show, best leave the second plate uneaten," Mia advised. "We want you fed, but too much food will slow you down."

Wade nodded. Mia and Sean, who owned and operated the local pub, had four children under the age of six. What had happened to Chester was every parent's worst nightmare. Not only would the O'Brians be fearing for the missing boy, but they'd be wondering if their own children were safe.

Which killed him. The safety of all the citizens of Curry County was Wade's top priority, but the children were in a special category of their own. Having one missing—and no clue who had him or why—was Wade's version of hell.

"Point taken, Mia. I'll be back to work shortly."

"I didn't mean that as a criticism, Wade. We've seen how hard you and your team are working. You should know that almost everyone I've spoken with today has taken part in the search effort, as much as they're able. The whole town is behind you."

"I appreciate that."

"And it looks like you won't have to eat alone after all." She nodded toward the door. Dougal had just stepped inside and was already heading this way. "I take it he's your dinner companion?"

"Yeah."

"Once you've found Chester and brought him home safe and sound, I suggest you move on to someone a little cuter, Sheriff."

"Very funny, Mia." These days it seemed almost everyone considered his love life—or lack thereof—fair game. Wade was not amused.

He stood to shake Dougal's hand, then waved him to the chair. "I ordered for you. Hope that's okay."

Mia had moved on to another table, and Dougal sank into the empty chair, staring at the food like it was the best thing he'd seen all day. "Awesome." He took a big bite of the burger and washed it down with half a glass of water. "This has been one hell of a day. And I mean that literally."

"Did you manage to write another chapter of the book?"

Dougal nodded, waiting until he'd swallowed to add, "Just sent it off to LibrarianMomma before I left to come here. Your timing was perfect. I can't remember the last time I felt so brain dead."

"Likewise." A minute ago, Wade had been starving.

Mia's well-intentioned reminder of how much the community was counting on him to find Chester, and apprehend the person responsible for his disappearance, had stolen his appetite.

Wade had never been one to take his responsibilities lightly.

"Do you really think Ed has Chester? Isn't it more likely he's taking advantage of the boy's disappearance to get you to write his story?"

"Tell me this—if Ed doesn't have Chester, then who the hell does? We don't have another suspect."

"It's still possible he's a runaway and afraid to come home." Wade hesitated, then added, "He could have had an accident as well."

"Chester's a smart kid. I can't see him doing anything too stupid."

"Well, we did follow up on a lead from Cory. She claimed she saw Chester talking to the football coach on Monday. So I just paid Brad Scott a visit."

"I remember that bozo. Why would he want to talk to Chester?"

"He claims he didn't. But I'm not sure I believe him. The man's life is in turmoil—he seems really stressed. Sometimes the end of a marriage and restricted access to children can send a man off the deep end."

"If he has a propensity for pedophilia, he might have acted on it in the past."

"He has no record. If he ever crossed that boundary with any of his students, no one ever reported it."

"So if his conversation with Chester was innocent, why is

he denying it?"

"It's possible Cory was confused and Chester was approached by someone else. I have a photograph I'm going to take over to Charlotte's place later. See if Cory can confirm Brad Scott was the coach she saw speaking to her brother. But even if it wasn't Scott, there's another angle to this story that has me suspicious."

Dougal was working on his fries now, and a twinge of Wade's original hunger stirred in his gut. Deciding it would be a shame to waste a free meal, he dipped some of his spiral fries into the ketchup.

"So what's the angle?"

"Do you remember Daisy being friends with Brad's wife, Sharleen, when they were younger?"

"When I think of Sharleen, all I remember are her huge boobs. Sorry—I guess that's sexist, but it's the truth."

"She's into fitness now. Skinny as a model, only with more muscles."

"You talking about Sharleen Scott?" Mia was back, this time with a couple of complimentary draft beers. "She teaches Zumba classes in the Anglican church basement on Monday, Wednesday, and Friday."

"You go to those classes, Mia?" Wade asked.

She looked at him incredulously. "You do remember I have four preschoolers, right? My mom is willing to babysit so I can work. But even that is getting too much for her."

"But you knew she taught the classes…" Wade wanted to keep her talking.

"Working in a pub, I learn a lot of stuff that isn't relevant to my own life."

"You were just a few years younger than us in high school," Dougal said. "Do you remember Daisy Hammond and Sharleen being friends?"

"More like rivals. They were both crazy about Kyle Quinpool."

Wade hadn't expected that. "But Sharleen started dating Brad in her junior year."

"Yeah, he was older—a big football star. You'd have expected him to be the best catch in town. But he wasn't nearly as good-looking as Kyle. Not half as charming, either." Mia sighed. "Not that either quality proved much help to Kyle in the end. It's so tragic the way things have turned out for him and his kids."

"Not to mention Daisy," Wade felt obliged to point out. She was, after all, the one who was dead.

"True. She was so pretty. And so good at getting whatever she wanted. At least until the twins were born. Motherhood was a rude shock to that woman."

"She had postpartum psychosis," Wade pointed out. "Her behavior at that time wasn't her fault." Back in the day, Wade, Dougal, Kyle, and Daisy had been close friends, and he felt obliged to defend her.

"Yeah, well, if I told Sean I was sleeping with another man because I had postpartum psychosis, I don't think he would be impressed."

Dougal's brows shot up. He glanced at Wade, then back at Mia. "You saying Daisy had an affair?"

Mia gave a knowing, slightly smug, nod.

No doubt being a purveyor of secrets was one of the pleasures of her job. But before Wade could give her the satisfaction of asking who the man in question was, Dougal had taken the required leap in logic.

"It was Brad Scott, wasn't it?"

"Yes. And trust me, Sharleen and Daisy weren't friends at all after that."

※

"Is Chester dead?"

The question dug into Charlotte's heart like a burr, with a pain that grew worse the more you probed. She set down her fork and looked across the table at the little girl who'd asked it.

Cory's head was lowered over her plateful of spaghetti—food she hadn't touched, even though it was her favorite meal.

"No." Honesty compelled Charlotte to add, "I don't believe so."

"But he's been gone a long time."

"Chester's pretty angry about your father being in prison. Maybe he's still too mad to come home." This might've been the best-case scenario at the moment, but despite Dougal's theory that his father had abducted him, Charlotte still clung to the possibility that Chester was a runaway with hope, if not optimism.

"Mrs. Field says everyone in Twisted Cedars has been looking for him, including the sheriff and all the police. If he was hiding I think someone would have found him by now."

"True, a lot of people are looking for your brother. But Chester's a smart kid. Could be he found a really good hiding spot."

"Maybe."

The word came out flat, devoid of hope.

Charlotte realized she shouldn't be surprised. After all, what basis did Cory have to expect a good outcome from this latest catastrophe in her life? Cory had been so young when she lost her mother. Then, months after her father remarried and it seemed she was going to be a part of a "regular" family, her mother's body had been found and her father—the only parent she'd ever really known—sent to prison.

This kid's life had been one disaster after another.

And when she'd ended up in Charlotte's care, what had Charlotte done? She'd farmed the kids out to an after-school sitter so she could continue to work at her beloved library.

It was a decision Charlotte now bitterly regretted.

If she'd thought more about the kids and less about herself, she would have given the mayor her resignation and devoted herself to the well-being of her sister's children. Charlotte had no doubt that if she'd been less selfish, Chester would still be here and Cory would be chatting with her mouth full, as usual, instead of looking like she had nothing left to live for.

But she couldn't say any of that to Cory.

And even if she could, it wouldn't help.

If only she could convince Cory to eat at least. "Not very hungry, huh? How about some milk?" Charlotte nudged the glass closer to her niece and felt a small measure of satisfaction when Cory took a couple of sips.

"I bet Chester's really hungry right now."

"He might be." It was better than speculating he was

dead. "Or maybe he's hiding in someone's summer cabin and he's found a whole bunch of potato chips and sodas the owners left in their cupboards."

Cory's lips twitched slightly. "At night he's probably sleeping in the biggest bed. And watching all their DVDs."

Charlotte left her chair and went to give Cory a hug. "We have to imagine the best right now, honey. It doesn't help Chester at all if we only think about the bad things."

"But—"

The front door opened, and Dougal called out, "Hello? Charlotte you in here?"

"Back in the kitchen."

She could hear footsteps on the plank flooring. Sounded like more than one person. Sure enough, Dougal appeared with Wade in his wake.

"I've got the sheriff with me."

That sounded official. She held her breath as she studied first one man's face, then the other's.

"Hey, Charlotte. Cory." Wade sounded—and looked—exhausted. "I'm here to ask some questions."

Charlotte suspected he was still in the uniform he'd been wearing yesterday when she'd reported Chester missing.

"You guys okay?" Dougal came to her, brushed back her hair so he could kiss her cheek.

The concern in his eyes made her want to cry. He was being so sweet to her when she knew how tough the past few days had been on him. She mustered a small smile.

"We're all right. Can I get you guys anything?" She pointed to the bowl of spaghetti Bolognese on the table. "We've got plenty of food."

Her offer was quickly declined.

"With your permission, I'd like to show Cory a couple photos," Wade said.

A disorienting memory flashed before Charlotte of another time Wade had stood in this room with her. They'd been talking about the future of their relationship and whether they'd be able to remain friends after he'd asked her to marry him and she'd turned him down. Funny how something that had seemed so important then could feel almost trivial now.

In the face of Chester's disappearance, nothing else seemed to matter.

"Sure, if you think it will help. But what's the picture of?"

"First one is Brad Scott, the high school football coach. He's the only football coach in town, but I need to confirm he was the man Cory saw talking to Chester last week."

Charlotte took one of her niece's hands. "You okay to look at the picture, Cory?"

"Yes." Cory's voice was so quiet only Charlotte heard her.

"You can show her the picture."

Wade nodded before stepping forward and laying the photo on the table beside Cory's almost full glass of milk. "Is this the man you saw talking to your brother, Cory?"

After just one quick glance, her niece frowned. "No."

"Are you sure?"

"This man is fat. The coach who talked to Chester was sort of regular sized." She turned to Dougal. "Like him."

Wade was expressionless as he removed the photo.

"Thanks, Cory. How about this man? Does he look like the guy?"

Charlotte looked over Cory's head at a mug shot of a man who had to be Dougal's father, Ed Lachlan.

"No," Cory said, sounding less certain this time. "That's not him, either."

"Okay." Wade smiled, as if the answers had been just what he was hoping for. "Thanks, Cory. You've been really helpful."

Charlotte glanced from him to Dougal, desperate to understand what this meant. Was it good or bad?

After a fruitless effort to coax her niece into eating more of her dinner, Charlotte gave Cory permission to watch TV in the family room. Cory scooted off thankfully.

When she was certain Cory couldn't hear her, Charlotte rounded on the two men. "What does this mean?"

"We can be pretty sure it wasn't Brad Scott who talked to Chester on Monday," Wade said. "But it's still possible it was Ed Lachlan. This is an old photo, plus it seems Ed is talented at disguising his appearance."

"If it was," Dougal continued, "he might have pretended to be a football coach in order to earn Chester's trust and establish a bond with him—to make abducting him a few days later that much easier."

Charlotte folded her arms in front of her chest, digging her nails into the soft skin of her forearms. It was so hard to believe the man who was Dougal's father was capable of such evil. "So Brad Scott is off the suspect list."

"Probably," Wade said. "Though he does have a surprising connection to the Quinpool family, so I'm not totally discounting him."

"What is the connection?"

Succinctly Wade gave her the highlights of his interview with Scott, his subsequent conversation with Scott's, wife Sharleen, and then Mia O'Brian's comments from the Linger Longer just moments ago.

Charlotte couldn't believe what this was adding up to. "So you think my sister had an affair with Brad Scott?"

"So far it hasn't been substantiated, but Mia sounded pretty certain," Wade said. "And if it was true, then it's possible Brad was still in love with Daisy, blamed Kyle for her death, and wanted to hurt Kyle by going after his son."

It sounded like a viable theory, but Charlotte was still in shock about her sister having an affair. "This is the first I've ever heard that Daisy cheated on Kyle."

"We only have Mia's gossip to go on," Dougal was quick to point out.

"I'll going to bring both Brad and Sharleen in for interviews," Wade said. "And then I'm going to drive out to the prison and talk to Kyle."

Charlotte had been thinking about Kyle a lot today. Whatever his faults, he did love his children. This situation had to be hell for him, too. "I assume he's been told about Chester going missing?"

"Yes," Wade replied.

"He must be going crazy." Charlotte had never liked her sister's husband much—mainly because he'd kept her at arm's length from her niece and nephew for so many years—but she did feel sorry for him now. She could imagine how helpless he would feel, finding out his son was missing and being unable to do anything to help find him.

"Yeah, I imagine. His father told me he was driving up to Salem for a visit with Kyle today. I might just stop in and talk to Jim tonight as well, see what he has to say about this alleged affair of Daisy's."

"I appreciate all you're doing, Wade. Can I at least make you a cup of coffee before you go?"

"Thanks for the offer, but we've got a pot on the go twenty-four seven at the office. And I should get moving."

Charlotte walked him to the back door, putting a hand on his arm and repeating her thanks. "I'd be going even crazier right now if I didn't know this investigation is in your hands."

"I won't stop until we find him," Wade promised.

But he didn't—couldn't—promise Chester would be okay when it happened.

chapter ten

WHEN CHARLOTTE RETURNED to the kitchen she found Dougal had put on a fresh pot of coffee.

"Hope you don't mind. That stuff they have at the sheriff's department is swill."

"Are you going back there tonight?"

For an answer, Dougal held out his phone so she could see the screen. A new message had arrived from LibrarianMomma: *Chapter two was good. Ready to work on the next one?*

"Why don't you put him off until the morning?" She brushed her hand over the lines on Dougal's forehead. Communicating so intensively with the father he hated was taking a toll. Plus, he had to be exhausted. Neither of them had been able to sleep much last night.

"I can't. I have to write this book as fast as humanly possible."

She swallowed at the grim look in his eyes. If Lachlan did have Chester, then he wouldn't let the boy go until he had what he wanted—the finished book. "Oh, Dougal. Don't most books take months, even years, to write?"

"I'm going to set a new world record with this one," Dougal promised.

Then he drew her into his arms, and she let her head drop to his shoulder. It felt so nice to be held. But even as she sighed and relaxed into his arms, her thoughts veered to Chester. There would be no one holding her nephew tonight, making him feel safe.

And even if Dougal gave Lachlan the book he wanted, the man was a vicious murderer. Could they count on him to keep his word and let Chester go?

Gently she disengaged from the embrace and went to get a travel mug from the cupboard. As she filled it with the freshly brewed coffee she asked, "Do you think there's a chance Wade might be right and Brad Scott is behind Chester's disappearance?"

"I suppose it's possible. I can see why Wade wants to investigate further."

Which alternative would be safer for Chester—Ed Lachlan or Brad Scott? It was a no-win scenario. She had to keep praying the answer was neither, that Chester was hiding somewhere, perfectly safe. But as each hour went by, that option seemed less likely.

"This is all my fault for not quitting my job and staying home with the twins."

"Hey. Stop that. Don't blame yourself."

"How can I not? When I think of all they've been through in their short lives, it just about kills me."

"Yes, it's unfair. And hard. But I can't see how any of it was your fault. Just the fact that you were willing to step in as their guardian makes you a damn good person in my opinion."

"It was the right thing to do. And it was what I *wanted*,

of course."

"Maybe. But it wasn't easy. So don't you beat yourself up. Working parents all across America rely on after-school care for their children."

"Yes. But maybe I should have hired an older child to escort them from school to Nola Thompson's house."

"It's only a few blocks, and the Thompson kids walk it all the time. If Chester was kidnapped, then whoever did it was going to find a way."

"You don't think there's a chance he's a runaway, do you?"

Dougal didn't meet her eyes. "I guess it's possible."

But she could hear in his voice that he didn't. "Be honest with me."

"I don't want to take away your hope. It's just—I have this really strong feeling that my old man took him. And until I find out otherwise, I have to keep writing that damn book as if Chester's life depends on me finishing as quickly as possible."

She wished she could relieve Dougal of this burden. But he was right. "Thank you. I know this is extremely tough on you."

"I've interviewed lots of criminals and murderers for my books. It's different when it's someone who's related to you, though. Who shares your DNA."

"Only fifty percent of your DNA," she reminded him, following him to the front door, where he paused to kiss her.

"I'll check in with you in a few hours," he promised.

She hated to see the bleak expression in his eyes.

"Don't let him get to you. His sins are not yours."

Dougal nodded, but she could tell her words didn't really reach him.

※

ON THE SHORT drive to Jim Quinpool's apartment, Wade reflected on what he knew of the man. He'd been a protective, somewhat indulgent father to his only child, Kyle, as well as an influential member of Twisted Cedar's business community. Not only did Jim own the most successful real estate business in the area, but he had also been active with the Chamber of Commerce.

Some of Wade's contemporaries—Dougal included—had been surprised when Kyle turned down a football scholarship to become his father's business partner. But not Wade. Kyle was the kind of guy who preferred being the large fish in the small pond. For him, staying in Twisted Cedars, marrying his high school sweetheart, and joining his dad's company had been the logical choice.

Successful business, beautiful wife, important standing in the community—until the birth of the twins, Kyle had led a charmed life, and Jim and Muriel had basked in their son's success.

But there was no doubt things had changed after Cory and Chester's arrival. Daisy had withdrawn, become depressed and incapable of looking after herself, let alone her babies.

The change in her behavior had been put down to postpartum psychosis—and Wade had the reports from her doctor to support that. No one knew if it was this illness or something else that had led Daisy to walk out on her husband and children a year later. Shortly after the divorce was finalized, she'd "disappeared" from town—or so everyone had thought.

Though Kyle was currently serving time for criminally negligent homicide, Wade didn't think anyone but Kyle—and possibly his parents—really knew what had happened the night Daisy died.

Undoubtedly there had been an argument—but about what? Kyle had claimed they were talking about custody of the twins. But could it have been the affair with Brad Scott?

On the face of it, none of this had anything to do with Chester's disappearance. But his father's arrest had definitely been responsible for Chester's frame of mind the day he went missing. Possibly someone had used his feelings of anger and abandonment for their own ends…whatever they might be.

Having reached Quinpool Realty, Wade went up the stairs to the second-floor apartment and rapped on the door. Jim answered immediately, in a state of obvious inebriation.

"Have you found my grandson?" he asked, words blurring into the background noise of the television.

"Not yet. I need to talk to you about some things." Wade could see an open bottle of Scotch on the low table by the sofa, one-third empty. "Mind if I come in?"

Jim didn't answer, just walked away from the door and grabbed the remote. It took him a few tries to hit the Mute button. "No sense talking to me. If I knew where Chester was, don't you think I'd go get him myself?"

"I'm wondering if there could be a connection between Chester's disappearance and your family troubles." The apartment had been finished with high-end materials—granite countertop and stainless-steel appliances in the adjacent kitchen. Good-quality furnishings and nice paintings on the walls.

But the place looked like hell. Not just messy, but actually dirty, to the point where a funky odor had developed. The condition of the apartment didn't compute with what Wade knew of Jim. Not that long ago he'd been one of the best-dressed men in town, with a beautiful Mercedes he kept in immaculate condition.

"Family troubles," Jim scoffed. "What would you know?"

"I know ten years ago you had the world by the tail. Devoted wife, successful business, son married and happy, one of the biggest houses in town…" Wade glanced around the condo. "Contrast that with now—your wife has left you, your business is closed, you live in a pigpen, and your son is in prison."

Jim glared, his eyes spilling anger and hatred. "It's all goddamned Daisy's fault. She was so spoiled, so used to being the center of attention, she couldn't handle the fact that the twins took the spotlight away from her."

"Her doctor diagnosed her with postpartum psychosis."

"Bullshit! She was the most selfish woman I've ever met. She deserted her own children!"

"And then she had that affair…"

"She had no shame," Jim agreed. "Sleeping with the very guy her husband—"

Abruptly he stopped, realizing he'd spoken thoughtlessly, admitted too much.

"Goddamn you, Wade. Why are you digging in my family's dirty laundry? This has nothing to do with Chester."

"No? You don't think it's possible the man who was sleeping with Daisy might be angry at Kyle for killing her?"

"Kyle didn't kill Daisy! It was a damned accident!"

"*Criminally negligent homicide* is what the courts call it. Either way, accident or homicide, it's because of Kyle that Daisy is dead. So maybe this man decides to get even by taking Chester."

Jim's eyes widened with fright. Clearly this possibility had never occurred to him. "Scott wouldn't do something like that. He has kids of his own."

Wade permitted himself a moment's satisfaction as the name he'd been probing for slipped easily off Jim's tongue. "The fact that Brad Scott has kids means he knows how much he'll hurt Kyle by taking Chester."

Jim let out a string of curse words. "Then what are you doing here? You need to haul Scott's ass into jail and get him talking."

"I've spoken to Scott. And to his wife. Right now I don't have a shred of evidence to suggest Scott kidnapped Chester."

"Then why the hell did you bring it up?"

"To illustrate a point. It's possible that the mistakes and tragedies connected with Daisy's death are also connected to Chester's disappearance. I need you to come clean with me. Tell me what really happened the night Daisy died."

Jim paced to the bottle on the table and topped up his glass with a shaking hand. "Kyle already told you everything. That's why he's in prison. To pay for his crimes."

"Maybe the reason he's in prison is just to avoid a trial."

"That's right. He didn't want to put his kids through all the hell of a court case."

"Or maybe he just didn't want to risk the truth coming out."

"That's crazy. Kyle told you exactly what happened that night. And I backed up every detail I could."

"Yes, you've been a very protective father. But you went too far this time."

"You're just speculating."

"Am I? Kyle told me he and Daisy were arguing about child-custody issues the night she died. But that wasn't true. They were fighting about her affair with Brad Scott. Kyle didn't like that much, did he?"

"What husband would?"

"They were no longer married at that point."

Jim looked like he wanted to leap across the room and grab Wade's throat. Instead he turned to the fireplace and a picture of his family taken during happier times, when he and Muriel were still married and the twins were about three years old.

"You keep twisting my words. I won't stand for it. I've got nothing else to say to you, Sheriff. Now, leave my home."

chapter eleven

June 15, 1972, Librarian Cottage outside of Twisted Cedars, Oregon

IT WAS TEN on a Sunday evening, a month after the first time Shirley heard the distinctive knock on her door, that she heard it again. Immediately she sensed it was him.

She'd just poured herself a cup of herbal tea, spilling a little in the saucer, to her annoyance. Recently she'd developed a fine tremor in her hands. Most annoying. Miss Marple, always so stalwart in tense situations, would not be impressed.

With each day that had passed since the young man first announced himself to her, Shirley had felt increasingly hopeful that having made his point with her, he would never return.

There had been the puzzling matter of her red scarf's disappearance, followed by the even more suspicious disappearance of the one she'd purchased to replace it.

But women lost scarves all the time. They were almost as tricky as gloves to keep track of.

She felt badly for the young man, of course, and for the boy he had been. But the unfortunate choice of his adoptive parents hadn't been hers. The best thing for him was to put the past out of his mind and concentrate on the future. That was what she had done. And it kept her sane.

Shirley sat at the table and sipped her tea, waiting for the second knock.

It didn't come.

This time she didn't even consider going for her gun. She was tough. But she wouldn't be able to shoot him. Not now.

So she waited. And when half an hour had passed in such silence that she began to wonder if she'd imagine the knock in the first place, she finally rose from her chair and opened the front door.

In the summer dusk she could see the shadows of the forest around her. Above, in the indigo-blue sky a single star sparkled. The air held only the sighs of the branches rustling in the faint breeze.

He could be hiding anywhere. He could have already left. Maybe he'd never even been here.

And then, as she was about to shut the door, she saw it—a glimmer on the front mat. Upon closer inspection she saw it was a snow globe.

She picked it up. It felt heavy in her hand. Inside the glass bubble was a miniature Main Street, and on the wooden base was inscribed Roseburg, Oregon. *Slowly she turned it over once, then again, sending bits of snow fluttering over the little shops, cars, and people inside the globe.*

Two weeks ago she'd gone to the State Library Association conference in Roseburg.

Did he know that? Was that why he'd purchased this for her?

After one last look down the road that led, eventually, to civilization, Shirley withdrew into her house. She carried the snow globe to a lamp, where she studied it more closely. There was no hidden message, nothing at all to suggest the boy had brought this for her.

She almost threw it away. She wanted no reminders, and just the sight of this made her skin crawl. But somehow she could not, so instead she placed it on the bottom shelf of her curio cabinet, where she would never see it unless she crouched down to her knees.

AT NINE THAT evening Wade held an impromptu meeting in the situation room with Marnie and Deputies Field, Carter, and Dunne. As he glanced around the table at his exhausted and discouraged team, he felt an unaccustomed sense of hopelessness.

"It's been over twenty-nine hours since Chester Quinpool disappeared, and so far we haven't found one piece of physical evidence. We have no idea if we're dealing with a runaway, an accident, an abduction, or a homicide."

"I hope this isn't your idea of a pep talk." Marnie was going around the table offering fresh coffee. Earlier she'd placed a plate of doughnuts at the center of the table. Of the assorted dozen, only two were left.

The team was already strung out on caffeine and sugar. Wade knew they couldn't keep operating at this level of intensity.

"It's reality," Wade countered. "Unless someone knows something I don't?"

He glanced at each team member individually. Not one spoke up.

"Right," Wade continued. "Until now we've been focusing on an intensive search and questioning of potential witnesses in town and within a ten-mile radius. It's time to widen the net and take a more systematic approach."

Again his words were met with a weary silence. The only sound Wade could hear was Carter, tapping his pen repetitively on his notepad, an anxious gesture betraying the highstrung state of his nerves.

"Carter, you'll be search operation coordinator for Curry County." Carter, with his physical stamina, would have the energy for the job. "It's time to pull out of the forest reserve around the Librarian Cottage and key in on campgrounds, state parks, recreational properties. With the summer season over, it's possible Chester could be hiding out in a nearby vacant cottage. Let's cover as many square miles as is physically possible, with copters where necessary."

"On it."

Wade turned to Deputy Dunn next. His eldest deputy's large frame was hunched over a stack of paperwork, and he was shuffling through the pages, as if hoping a magical clue would leap off one of the pages.

"Dunn, you'll be our on-site coordinator supervising change of command, coordinating with the county and state departments and agencies, responding to investigative inquires and gathering intelligence."

The most senior officer in the department, Dunn sometimes took umbrage at being assigned duties without consultation, but tonight he just nodded his assent.

"I've asked the state police for help in case this turns into a homicide investigation, and they're coordinating an Oregon-wide search as well. Field, you'll remain liaison with

Chester's family as well as manage our media relations. Marnie can help you with that. She's already got some stuff up on Facebook and Twitter, that sort of thing." Wade was a little vague on the details of social media, but he knew he could count on Marnie to sort it out.

Next Wade filled the team in on the conversation Cory had seen her brother have with an older man who appeared to be a football coach. He told them about his discussions with Brad Scott, his wife, and Jim Quinpool.

"I'm going to drive to Salem tomorrow to question Kyle," Wade concluded. "At this point I'm grasping at straws, but I want to make sure Chester's disappearance isn't connected to his mother's death or his father's subsequent incarceration."

There was some trivial chitchat after this, which Wade quickly put a halt to.

"I expect the overtime is going to continue for the foreseeable future, or until we find our boy," Wade said. "With that in mind, I want each of you to grab some sleep tonight. To borrow an analogy from Carter, this is no longer a sprint, it's a marathon."

Five minutes later the only one left in the room with Wade was Marnie. She was collecting the dirty coffee cups and brushing doughnut crumbs off the table.

"Leave that for the cleaning crew. You should get some rest."

"I napped a few hours this afternoon," she admitted. "That couch in your office is pretty comfortable."

"You took a nap in my office?"

"Why not? It was the only quiet place in the building."

She put her hands on her hips, a combative posture she seemed to take quite often around him. "You don't object, do you?"

He couldn't think of a logical reason why he should. And yet later, when he returned to his office contemplating zoning out himself for a bit, it seemed he could still see the indent of Marnie's petite, curvy body in the old leather cushions.

So he drove home instead, where he followed a two-hour sleep with a long shower and a proper breakfast of eggs, toast, and orange juice. The drive to Salem took him four and a half hours, and he arrived at the start of opening hours for the Oregon State Penitentiary.

Kyle had lost some weight and his skin had turned sallow, but he held his head high as he walked to the other side of the table and took his seat across from Wade.

"Have you found my son yet?"

His tone grated, reminding Wade of the Kyle he'd known in high school. Anytime he was caught out for doing something wrong, he immediately went on the offensive. That quality had made him a great football player. It didn't serve him quite as well now.

"When we find Chester, you'll be one of the first to hear about it. We're doing everything we can. I came here because I'm hoping you can help."

"You get me out of here, and I'd love to. It's killing me to be stuck in here when my son needs me."

"We've got a lot of manpower working this investigation," Wade assured him. On this point he couldn't help but sympathize with his old friend. "But we could use more information. Has it occurred to you that Chester's disappearance might be related to you and the crimes that put you in here?"

"What the hell do you mean by that?"

"I mean I would like the truth. You told me you and Daisy were fighting about custody of the twins the night she died. But I believe you were really arguing about her affair with Brad Scott. Isn't that right?"

As Wade stared calmly, directly into Kyle's eyes, he could almost see the other man's inner squirming.

"What? How did you—"

"How did I find out about that? During routine questioning as I was looking for your son." Wade planted his hands on the table and leaned in. "What else have you lied about, Kyle?"

"Nothing important. I can't see why it matters to you why Daisy and I were arguing. I readily admit that I pushed her. Harder than I meant to, obviously."

"There are times when so-called white lies are acceptable. Homicide investigations do not qualify."

"Fine. You caught me out." Kyle leaned back in his chair. "Yes, Daisy was sleeping with Brad Scott. And yes, I wasn't pleased. Satisfied now?"

"Anything else in your story you want to modify?"

Kyle set his jaw and didn't add a word.

His original story was that his parents and children had been asleep upstairs during the argument and only after Daisy had been pushed into the wall, struck her head on the corner, and died had his father come down to see what was going on.

But Wade was no longer prepared to accept that version.

"How about your claim that the two of you were alone when you pushed Daisy? If you were having a loud argument, surely at least one of your parents would have woken up and come to see what was going on."

Kyle remained mute, though his eyes shone with resentful anger.

Wade pushed harder. "You weren't alone when you pushed her. Who else was in the room?"

Kyle's gaze shifted slightly to the left as he spit out, "No one."

Wade leaned forward. "That's a lie."

"Where's your proof?"

Up until that moment Wade had been confident Kyle was responsible for Daisy's death, a conclusion borne out by the fact that Kyle and Jim had taken Daisy's body out to the Librarian Cottage and buried it in an unused vegetable plot.

But in the moment of that slight hesitation and shifting of Kyle's eyes, it occurred to Wade that not only was Kyle not alone when he pushed Daisy—but quite possibly he hadn't done the pushing at all.

Which meant Kyle had gone to prison to protect someone else.

Kyle was generally out for number one. But the Quinpools had always been tight. On more than one occasion Wade had seen Jim put his arm proudly around his son and say, *We Quinpools watch out for one another.*

Could it be his father Kyle was protecting? That might explain why Jim was drinking so heavily. The burden of guilt, knowing his son was serving time on his behalf would be extreme.

"You could be hurting your son by keeping these secrets, Kyle."

"What's happened to Chester has nothing to do with Daisy's death. Instead of wasting your time here, you should be out looking for my boy, Wade." Kyle kept his voice low, even though he was pulsing with rage. "He's a good kid. You better find him before anything bad happens to him, or I swear, when I get out of here—"

"Don't compound your problems by threatening an officer of the law." Wade stood, more than a little angry himself. "If you change your mind and decide to cooperate in our efforts to find Chester, get in touch."

Kyle's hands were in fists, his jaw clenched and his eyes flashing murder. But he didn't respond.

chapter twelve

WHEN HER CELL phone rang shortly after lunch on Friday, Charlotte's heart went into palpitations. Even though the chime was the unique one she'd assigned to Dougal, she couldn't help the illogical hope it might be Chester calling. No doubt her nerves were fried from too little sleep and proper food, combined with too much worry and caffeine.

But of course it wasn't Chester.

She tried not to sound downcast as she said, "Hi, Dougal. How are things going?"

"Just finished a marathon session with Ed." Exhaustion permeated each slowly spoken word. "He's giving me an hour to make notes, and then he wants me to check into yet another chat room again at two o'clock."

Charlotte wished Dougal could tell Ed to screw off. Nothing was worth putting the man she loved through this anguish. Except, of course, something was. Chester's life.

The faster Ed told his story, the sooner Chester would be free. At least that was Dougal's contention, and Charlotte was beginning to think that he was right.

"Stella was in to clean today. It was nice having company." Stella's younger partner, Liz Brooks, should have been there, too, but she'd taken time off for a trip, and Charlotte had been just as glad. She found Stella very comforting to be around. Liz, not so much.

"I'm sorry I haven't been there for you."

"I didn't mean to complain. This is hell for you, too. I get that." Charlotte paced around the kitchen island, trailing her fingers on the freshly oiled butcher block. Stella used a special beeswax cream that made the kitchen smell of vanilla.

It seemed wrong for her home to be so pristine when her world was so messed up and crazy. She still found it unbelievable that Chester had vanished so quickly and completely. Shouldn't there be at least one tiny clue left behind?

"Give Jamie a call," Dougal suggested. "I bet she'd be happy to keep you company for a while."

"She has work."

"Yeah. But she loves Chester, too. I bet she isn't getting much done at the accounting firm."

Dougal was probably right about that, but once he'd ended their call Charlotte didn't dial his sister the way he'd suggested. Instead, she went to the study and pulled out a pad of paper.

Just a year ago, she'd thought Twisted Cedars was a nice town, a place where accidents and heartbreaks happened but nothing truly evil.

But the events of the past few months had proven her wrong.

There had been so many tragic happenings these past few months. Everyone kept saying it was awful luck for the Quinpools. But it seemed to Charlotte that the tragedies involved her family, the Hammonds, just as much, if not more.

Was it possible all the problems sprang from the same root cause?

Charlotte started a list:

1. Daisy's death (homicide) and illegal burial—Kyle Quinpool
2. Four murdered librarians—Ed Lachlan
3. Aunt Shirley's suicide—possibly Ed Lachlan had a hand in this too?
4. Joelle Carruther's amnesia—accidental, caused by truck crash
5. Joelle's daughter's murder—possibly Ed Lachlan
6. Joelle Carruther's suicide/homicide—possibly Ed Lachlan
7. Chester's disappearance—possibly Ed Lachlan

Charlotte studied the list. Had she forgotten anything? Other bad things had happened—her parents' death in a car accident two years ago, for instance. But that had been an accident, and she was looking for tragedy combined with malicious intent.

The doorbell interrupted her focus, and she dropped her pen with a gasp.

Was it news?

A moment later Jamie called out. "It's just me, come to visit. Okay if I let myself in?"

"Of course." Dougal must have guessed she wouldn't call his sister and done it on her behalf. She put a hand on her heart. She had to stop being so jumpy. "I'm in the study."

A few seconds later, so was Jamie. She was dressed nicely for work, had done her hair and makeup, yet the dark circles under her eyes spoke of her own suffering. "How are you holding out?"

"I'm holding." Charlotte stood to give Jamie a hug. It felt surprisingly good. Despite being close in age she and Jamie had never been friends. Charlotte was very open to that changing. "And you?"

"I'm trying to work, but I can't think straight. I keep wondering if Dougal is right, if Brian Greenway *was* our father, and if so, if there was something I could have done to stop him—before he took Chester."

"So I'm not the only one who feels guilty. I blame myself for going back to work instead of taking the kids to and from school myself. Hell, maybe I should have homeschooled them."

"They would have hated that," Jamie said firmly. "And of course you went back to work. Do you think their father ever considered quitting the real estate business and staying home with them full-time?"

Jamie noticed the pad of paper then. "What's this?"

Charlotte moved the pen so Jamie could read the entire list.

"I think better when I write things down. So many awful things have happened recently. I was wondering if somehow they're all related."

"The librarians weren't from Twisted Cedars. But if we look at the names on this list—forgetting who is victim and who perpetrator—they all fall into either my family or yours."

She was right. "Daisy, Shirley, and Chester are all Hammonds."

"While Ed, Joelle, and her baby are from my family." Jamie circled her father's name. "And he's the link, isn't he?"

"How do you mean?"

"Well, he sort of belongs to both families. Since Shirley was his mother."

"That's true," Charlotte said. "I wonder who his father was, whether it might help to know."

"It couldn't hurt. Do you have any ideas?"

"Everyone who would have known is dead now—except Stella, I suppose. But I wonder if we could puzzle it out on our own. Shirley was fifteen and then sixteen years old when she had her baby. I've got family photo albums going back that far."

Jamie snapped her fingers. "Good thinking. Maybe we'll find a picture of her with a boyfriend. If we do, I'm sure Stella will be able to recognize him. Stella knows pretty much everyone in Twisted Cedars."

It felt good to be doing something proactive for a change, and Charlotte eagerly pulled several of the older photo albums out of the cabinet, leaving behind the newer albums, which she'd shown the twins just a few weeks ago. It was painful to recall just how excited Cory—and even Chester—had been to see photos of their mother as a child and adolescent.

Charlotte checked the date on the first page of the oldest album. "This looks like it should be the right one. It starts in 1932, which is when my dad's parents were married."

She and Jamie settled next to each other on the sofa. The book was large enough to rest half on Charlotte's lap and half on Jamie's. The chronologically organized photos had been mounted with sticky black corners, some of which had dried and lost their adhesiveness. As a consequence, they had to turn the pages very slowly, careful to keep the pictures in their proper places.

The album began with a single photograph taken at Charlotte's paternal grandparents' wedding. The newlyweds looked at the camera a little anxiously. Under the photo Grandmother Hammond had written *John and me on our wedding day.*

"Don't you just love old photo albums? Isn't it amazing to think of your grandmother writing these words almost a hundred years ago?"

Charlotte considered the question. A curious byproduct of being adopted was that while she'd loved the Hammonds as much as if they were her real parents, she didn't feel the same connection with the Hammond ancestors.

"I never knew any of my grandparents that well. My parents were older when they had Daisy, and they adopted me four years later when Dad was forty-five and Mom forty-three."

"That does seem old. Especially in those days."

A few self-conscious poses of the honeymoon couple in New York City were followed with pictures of them standing on the front porch of their first, and only, home, the very house Charlotte lived in today.

There had been improvements to the house since then, of course, including new siding and a cedar shake roof, but it did give Charlotte a shiver to think of all the family history and secrets this house must've held.

By the time the Hammonds had their first child, Shirley, the photographs were in color. There was a professional portrait, large enough to cover one entire page, of Shirley at age two.

"What an angel. Look at those blonde curls and blue eyes!" Jamie tilted her head. "Your sister looked a lot like her, didn't she?"

"She did." There was no question Daisy, like Shirley, had been lovely to look at, and at times it hadn't been easy being the plainer, younger, *adopted* sibling. To her credit, Charlotte's mother had always done her best to bolster her youngest daughter's self-esteem.

Charlotte remembered once her mother had actually said, *There can be such a thing as being too pretty. You end up attracting the wrong sort of attention.*

It had seemed a strange opinion at the time. Now Charlotte wondered if something specific had been behind it.

They flipped through pages documenting the birth of the Hammonds' son, Jonathon—John for short, after his father. This was followed by pictures of the children's grade school years, which all seemed perfectly normal. As Shirley matured they began to study the pictures more closely.

Shirley had grown even more beautiful in her teenaged years. She had a willowy figure and stood a little taller than most of her friends at her birthday parties. There was a noticeable gap in photographs after Shirley turned fifteen. The next photo taken was of her and her date the night of her high school graduation. It was the first time any boy had been included in a photo with Shirley—in this case a tall, nerdy fellow with horn-rimmed glasses and protruding front teeth.

"She would have been eighteen here," Jamie observed after exclaiming over Shirley's pink tulle dress. "A few years after she had the baby."

Charlotte tried to peer into the eyes of the girl in the photograph, but the poor resolution made it impossible to guess at any hidden depths. Shirley had been through so much by this point, but here she looked like just another happy, pretty teenaged girl.

"I suppose it's possible this boy was the father of her baby."

"It's the only clue we have," Jamie agreed.

Carefully Charlotte moved the photograph from the album. She found a protective envelope in one of the desk drawers and placed it carefully inside. "Next time I see Stella, I'll ask her if she knows who he is."

"I could show it to her tonight, if you're okay lending me the photo. I'm having her over for dinner. She wanted to see my new place."

Charlotte passed her the envelope. "How are you liking your new house?"

Jamie shrugged. "The place is great, but I still feel like a mess. I'd hoped a new environment would help me make a fresh start." She glanced down at her left hand, more specifically the finger that for a short time had sported an engagement ring and, for an even shorter period of time, a wedding band. "But it isn't that easy. And with Chester missing, nothing feels right."

"I'm sorry." She wished she could think of something more helpful to say.

"I didn't mean to complain. Especially since this is just as hard for you, if not harder." Jamie's gaze went to the photo of Daisy on the bookshelves.

Charlotte smiled. "That's one of my favorites of Daisy." She had taken the picture, actually, on a day about a year before her sister's marriage to Kyle, when their parents had been away. Daisy hadn't wanted to cook, so they'd ordered pizza and watched movies until very late. It had been one of a very few occasions when the two of them had had fun together.

"It is a nice photo," Jamie agreed. "But I should get going. I have to pick up some groceries before going home to cook. Are you going to be okay?"

"Cory should be home any minute." Charlotte had been keeping one eye on the time ever since she'd finished lunch. She knew it was best for Cory to keep her usual routines, but she couldn't help worrying whenever her niece wasn't under the same roof as her.

"Do you have to pick her up from school?"

"Her best friend's mother is doing that. Bailey Landax." Charlotte would have loved an excuse to escape the house for a few minutes. But she needed to be here for Chester. Just in case.

"Bailey's the Realtor who sold me my house." Jamie tucked the envelope containing the photo into her purse. "I felt a bit guilty using my—using Kyle's competitor."

"You had no choice. Quinpool Realty is probably going to remain closed as long as Kyle is incarcerated. I can't see his father running it again on his own."

"Probably not." Jamie gave her a hug. "You're sure you'll be okay?"

"I'm fine. But thanks for dropping in. You'll let me know if Stella recognizes the boy with Shirley?"

"Right away," Jamie promised.

Charlotte walked Jamie out the back door in order to avoid the reporters camped out at the front. Fortunately she could usually get a bit a privacy on her back porch, and she settled there now in one of the wicker chairs.

The fresh air felt good, and with the warm sun on her body, Charlotte was almost asleep when her cell phone rang. She pulled it out of her jeans pocket frantically. "Hello?"

"Charlotte, this is Bailey."

She hadn't expected it to be Chester, but she felt disappointed all the same. "Are you still okay to pick up Cory?"

"I'm at the school right now with Paige. The problem is Cory. She's not here. You didn't ask someone else to pick her up, did you?"

"No. *No.*" A voice inside Charlotte's head started shrieking. *This can't be happening! God, no, not Cory, too!* She struggled to stay calm and rational. "Have you spoken to her teacher?"

"Yes. Mrs. Young said Cory was definitely in class when the final bell rang. But after that...she just disappeared."

chapter thirteen

April 6, 1975, Librarian Cottage outside of Twisted Cedars, Oregon

*F*OUR YEARS HAD *passed since Shirley Hammond's illegitimate son had shown up on her doorstep. She never heard from him anymore, except once a year when a few days or weeks after attending the Oregon Library Association Conference, there would be a knock at her door.*

She never rushed to open the door and was always mildly relived to find no one standing on the other side when she did.

By now she'd come to expect the object that would be set out for her on the welcome mat. It would be a snow globe, a tacky souvenir from whatever Oregon city had hosted the conference for that year.

The first one, in 1972, had been from Roseburg, followed by Pendleton in 1973 and Corvallis in 1974.

This year, the snow globe would be from Medford, no doubt, the host city of the 1975 conference.

A few days after receipt of this gift she'd come home to discover another of her red scarves had "disappeared."

The pattern seemed innocuous enough. But it was baffling.

On this April day of 1975, Shirley stood for a long time on her front porch, alternately examining the snow globe she'd just picked up and studying the surrounding woods. He always arrived so silently, so he must've either walked or ridden a bike.

Which meant he might've still been out there. Watching her.

Why, she had no idea, and she didn't like speculating about it, either. Four years ago she made up her mind she wouldn't let him frighten her. Unfortunately, though, that was easier said than accomplished. She couldn't deny that over the years, a feeling of dread had been building inside her.

Even now, she felt a sliver of it slide down her back from her neck to her tailbone.

And that made her angry.

"What do you want from me?" she shouted out to the woods.

She waited several minutes for an answer, but none came.

Eventually she returned inside, clicking shut the new dead bolt she'd had installed last year. She hesitated, then added the snow globe to the others on the bottom shelf of her cabinet. She then tried to put the whole thing out of her mind by rereading one of her favorite Miss Marple mysteries, The Body in the Library.

For once, however, her old friend let her down. She couldn't sink into the story as she liked to do. And her favorite quote from the book, one that always made her chuckle, this time seemed in bad taste:

"What I feel is that if one has got to have a murder actually happening in one's house, one might as well enjoy it, if you know what I mean."

Tonight Shirley couldn't see the humor in that at all.

AFTER HIS INTERVIEW with Kyle Quinpool, Wade picked up lunch at a burger drive-thru, then immediately started back for Twisted Cedars. The long drive gave him an opportunity that had been rare for him lately—time to think.

In the back of his mind it had occurred to Wade that Kyle might have organized a friend or cohort to kidnap his son. It was a far-fetched scheme but one Wade had felt duty bound to check out. It was no secret Kyle hadn't wanted Charlotte to gain custody of his children. He'd pleaded for his soon-to-be ex-wife, Jamie, to take them, or at least his father or mother.

But the courts had chosen Charlotte, the sister of the wife who, in Kyle's mind at least, had caused all of his problems.

So, yeah, Wade figured Kyle had motive.

But why take Chester and not Cory?

Besides, Kyle's concern about Chester today had felt absolutely sincere.

Which meant Wade was no closer to finding out what had happened to the boy.

Or even if he was still alive.

Wade liked to believe an enterprising boy of nine could probably survive on his own for quite a while if he happened to stumble onto a winterized cottage stocked with provisions. Certainly the nice weather was in his favor.

This was, by far, Wade's most hopeful scenario. If indeed Chester was hiding out somewhere, one of the searchers would eventually find the boy. Chester could have traveled only so far on his bike. In another week or two, he was bound to be discovered.

The other possibilities were far grimmer. If he'd met with an accident—or been murdered—his body would probably turn up eventually. But it might not.

Then there was the third possibility. That he'd been abducted. Possible suspects here included a total stranger, Brad Scott, or Ed Lachlan.

Of them all, Ed seemed the most chilling proposition.

Ed had killed his second wife. And if Dougal was to be believed, he'd also killed four librarians—possibly five—as well as Joelle Carruthers and her daughter, Josephine. A man like that obviously had little regard for human life.

In fact, if he'd taken Chester, the boy might already be dead.

It was a brutal possibility but one that had to be considered. Wade didn't—couldn't—dwell on it, however. He had to believe that Chester was alive and that he would be found. Soon.

As Wade drove farther away from Salem, radio reception became spotty, and he switched from his favorite country music station to the CD of Chopin's nocturnes his mother had given him a long time ago.

The beautiful music was soothing, not because Wade was such a huge classical-music buff, but because it brought back the memories and sensation of his childhood, when he and his father would sit on the back porch and listen to his mother play.

So much of what had been good about his childhood—and it mostly had been good—was captured in those early morning concerts. As a boy he'd been proud and impressed with his mother, but he'd also been filled with anticipation for what was to come. A day of fishing with his dad, then home for a big Sunday dinner and some family time watching television together.

Such simple stuff.

But Wade remembered it all fondly.

Soon he was driving along the coast, and the beauty of the September day seemed to belie all the terrible things that had happened in Twisted Cedars this summer. Wade wondered if the pressures of his job would be easier to handle if he had a wife and children. He'd always figured he'd have both by this age.

For years he'd figured Jamie Lachlan was the right woman for him. But then she'd married Kyle, and he'd transferred his affections to Charlotte. That relationship had only lasted until Dougal moved back to town.

Was the universe trying to send him a message? Maybe he was the kind of guy who was better off single?

Wade was only ten minutes from town when a call came in from Marnie.

Normally Marnie opened every conversation—whether in person or over radio or phone—with a teasing comment or a jibe. Not this time. Her voice was taut as she said, "Charlotte Hammond just called in a 911. Her niece, Cory, went missing after school today."

Adrenaline jolted Wade into high alert. He glanced at the time display on the dash: 3:45.

"What happened?"

"Cory's best friend's mother—who happens to be Bailey Landax—was supposed to pick up Cory and her own daughter, Paige, after school. Several other mothers have already confirmed Bailey was on time, waiting right by the door when the bell sounded. But when the children came out, Cory wasn't among them."

An image of Cory's sad little face that last time he'd seen her flashed through Wade's mind, followed by intense grief mixed with anger. He struggled to tamp down the emotions, to remain focused and logical. "You're sure Cory was in class?"

"Her teacher, Olivia Young, insists she spoke to Cory just minutes before the final bell sounded. She'd noticed Cory seemed especially distraught that afternoon, and she'd asked if Cory wanted to talk about anything."

Immediately questions came to mind, but Wade shelved them for the moment. This first hour was crucial. "We need to get right on this. Immediately."

"Done, Sheriff. Deputy Dunne is at the school right now supervising a search of the school and questioning the other students and teachers. Carter's patrolling the area, and Field's going door to door in the neighborhood around the school." Marnie's voice dipped lower. "Should I put out an Amber Alert and notify the media?"

Wade hesitated. "I'd hold off for thirty minutes. Has anyone questioned Cory's friend, Paige?"

"I imagine Dunne is doing that right now."

"Okay. Good." Wade thought about Charlotte, how frantic she must've been. But in his gut Wade didn't believe Cory had been abducted by the same person who'd taken Chester.

For one thing, security at the school was tighter than ever since Cory's brother's disappearance. It would be very difficult for any attempted kidnapper to gain access to Cory when she was attending class. All the school exits were locked from the outside except the main door, and the school secretary was policing that.

If the teacher had indeed spoken to Cory just before the bell rang and if Cory hadn't been among the students leaving the main exit at three thirty, the most likely option was that she had slipped out one of the back doors, which were not locked from the outside, obviously, due to fire safety rules.

Wade tried to put himself into Cory's shoes. Clearly she was worried sick about her brother. Chester had told her he wanted to run away—maybe she had a secret idea where he might be and had gone to check it out.

Wade could think of one obvious spot she might go.

The Quinpools' home on Fifth Street was about five long blocks from school. The pretty two-story Victorian had been vacant since Kyle was arrested in late July. The home had been extensively searched several times over since Chester's disappearance, but Cory wouldn't know that.

Since Jim Quinpool had the keys, Wade called him and arranged to pick him up out front of his apartment on Driftwood Lane.

Sixty seconds after he terminated the call, Wade arrived and found Jim, unwashed and unshaven, standing none too steadily on the curb.

It was difficult to believe that just five years ago this man had been one of the pillars of the Twisted Cedars business establishment.

Not only could Jim pass for a homeless man in appearance, he also smelled like one as he climbed into the passenger side of Wade's SUV.

Wade unrolled his window and waited for the man to buckle up before he started driving.

"I can't believe Cory's gone now, too," Jim muttered. "Since you were elected sheriff this town's sure gone to hell."

"That's a fine observation from a man whose son is currently locked up for homicide. Especially if that son is serving time for a crime that *you* committed."

Wade glanced at Jim's face, which seemed to freeze for a few seconds before he shot back a retort of his own. "Goddam it, man. Would you stop barking up that tree and concentrate on finding my grandkids?"

"That's what I'm doing," Wade replied calmly.

Jim said nothing after that, and less than a minute later they arrived at the attractive two-story clapboard that had been the Quinpools' home for as long as Wade could remember. As kids he, Dougal, and Daisy had visited here often. Muriel Quinpool had given them the run of the basement. She hadn't been the sort of mother to check up on them on the guise of bringing them cookies or to question them excessively on their way in or out of the place.

They both got out of the SUV and stood on the sidewalk a moment, examining the home. While the lawn had been recently mowed and the flowerbeds were free of weeds, it still had a deserted feel to Wade.

"You keeping up the place?"

"I hired a kid down the street."

That figured. Jim wasn't the type to soil his own hands with manual labor. Wade tried the door to make sure it was still locked, then held out his hand for the keys.

"Just a minute." Jim started walking around to the backyard, and after a moment Wade followed. Once there, Jim checked the garden shed and then looked up into the branches of the tall oak trees.

"Those kids love climbing trees," he explained.

Wade looked, too. "Well, no one's up there right now."

"Let me check one last thing." Jim went to the back deck and picked up a decorative concrete rabbit. Upon close inspection, Wade saw it had been constructed with a hidden compartment in the base. Jim opened it up, then showed him.

It was empty.

"Spare key is gone," Jim said.

"Does the kid you hired to do the lawns know about the hidden key?"

"Nope. Kyle put that key there for the twins, in case they ever locked themselves out."

Wade could feel the band of pressure around his chest loosen. "Let's look inside."

Jim unlocked the back door which led to the kitchen. The room was spotless, except for an open package of chocolate chip cookies on the counter. Wade took a closer look. The entire first row of cookies was missing.

"Cory? This is Sheriff MacKay. I'm here with your grandpa. Everyone is really worried about you."

"Come out, honey," Jim added. "You won't be in any trouble. We just want to know you're safe."

No answer.

Wade glanced at Jim. "I'll check the main floor and upstairs. You take the garage and the basement."

After a quick nod, Jim headed for the stairs, calling out his granddaughter's name one more time as well as more assurances that she shouldn't be afraid.

Wade made quick work of the living and dining areas, the front entry, powder room, and study. Then he headed upstairs and worked his way through the rooms along the main landing. First was the main bedroom with en suite bathroom and walk-in closet.

Next, judging by the pastel color scheme and the few books and stuffed animals that had been left behind, was Cory's room. Wade had been almost certain he would find the little girl here, but everything was immaculate. Even the covers on the bed looked freshly ironed. Still Wade searched every possible nook and cranny two times over before giving up and moving on to Chester's room.

Football posters covered the walls in this room, which was also tidy, but unlike Cory's room, the bed covers were rumpled, and Wade spotted cookie crumbs on the carpet.

He didn't bother looking further.

"Hey, Cory. Did you come here looking for your brother?"

After about thirty seconds her head popped out from under the bed. "Yeah. But he isn't here."

chapter fourteen

Wednesday, April 7, 1975, Twisted Cedars Library, Oregon

IT WAS FIVE minutes before closing, and the library was deserted when Shirley decided to call a colleague from Medford she'd met during the annual conference. Isabel Fraser was an impressive librarian in her midforties who'd given a talk on the impact computers were going to have on the modern library. When Shirley had expressed a special interest in the subject Isabel had invited her to call so they could talk further, after the bustle of the conference was over.

Shirley was looking forward to becoming better acquainted with Isabel and to learning more about the future for her profession. As much as Shirley was a fan of tradition, she also loved being on the cutting edge of new technologies. Anything that encouraged more reading and distribution of knowledge was a plus in her book.

She was disappointed when Isabel didn't pick up her phone and the call was routed back to the switchboard.

"Medford Public Library. Terri speaking. May I ask who's calling?"

"This is Shirley Hammond from the Twisted Cedars Library. I was hoping to talk to Isabel Fraser. We met at the conference two weeks ago."

There was a long silence, and then the woman on the other end of the line said, "I'm sorry, but we've had a terrible tragedy here. I'm afraid Isabel has...passed away."

Shirley could make no sense of that. "But she wasn't that old. And she certainly didn't seem sick. Was it an accident?"

"No." The woman made a sound that might have been a gulp. "Isabel was murdered. Here. In the library basement. The police figure she died shortly after we closed for the night."

Shirley stared at the book stacks around her, feeling suddenly vulnerable. She was pretty sure she was alone in here—wasn't she? She got up and locked the front door. "How did it happen?"

"I'm sorry. It's pretty gruesome. Are you sure you want to hear?"

"I think I must."

"Isabel was strangled. Of all things by a red silk scarf. Nothing was stolen. And Isabel wasn't...defiled. No one has any idea what the motive could have been."

Shirley's heart almost stopped at the mention of a red silk scarf.

Could it be hers, one of the ones that had gone missing?

No. This had to be a coincidence.

Suddenly she thought of the snow globe.

Such a silly trinket. Why would he go to all that trouble to deliver it to her...unless maybe they had never been intended as souvenirs of her conferences but of something much darker.

"I—I have to go." The woman on the other line—Terri—had started speaking again, but Shirley hung up the phone anyway.

She went back to her desk and unlocked the bottom drawer. Inside was her purse as well as a large manila envelope containing contributions for the Library Improvement Fund. She *removed her purse but left the envelope where it was.*

She had to go home and think.

But then she heard a rustling sound from the mystery section. A chill tingled up her spine and over her scalp... She considered turning and running for the door. But that would be cowardly. And she was anything but a coward.

"Who's there?"

For a long time there was no answer. Tentatively she took a few forward steps. "The library's closed now. It's time for you to leave."

Still no answer. Had she imagined the noise? Perhaps the shocking news about Isabel Fraser had unhinged her.

Deciding she had to look or she'd spend the entire night worrying, Shirley made herself stride purposefully down to the end of one aisle, then across the back of the room to the mystery section. She was almost at the far wall, where a door led to the basement, when someone grabbed her from behind, one arm clasping her waist tightly, the other blocking her mouth and nose.

"We meet again," said a familiar voice, "Mother."

CHARLOTTE COULDN'T STOP hugging her niece any more than she could stop the happy tears streaming down her face.

"Thank you so much, Wade." She pressed her cheek to the top of Cory's head, so reassured that her niece was safe and home again.

"Happy to do my job," Wade replied.

Charlotte could see the worry still etched on his forehead. Not for a moment had he forgotten that there was still a child missing.

Cory eased out of her aunt's embrace, then mumbled, "I'm sorry for running away after school."

"It's okay." Charlotte gave her another hug. "It was a smart idea to check your house for Chester. But next time you have another smart idea like that, tell me and we'll look together."

"I thought maybe he was hiding from everyone else but he would come out for me."

"He probably would come out for you. We just have to find the right hiding spot." Wade had told her that his deputies were fanning out from town, searching all the deserted cottage homes in an ever-widening radius from town. Charlotte wanted to believe that her nephew was a simple runaway, that the nice weather and his good fortune in happening upon a well-stocked, unoccupied cottage was the reason he'd been gone so long.

There were stretches of time—some as long as ten minutes—where she managed to convince herself.

Once Wade was gone, Charlotte offered to order in pizza for dinner. To her surprise Cory seemed unenthused.

"My stomach hurts. I think I ate too many cookies."

Wade had explained about the cookies and how they'd given Cory away, so Charlotte didn't begrudge her niece a single one.

"When I've had too much junk food I like to have a drink of water, then brush my teeth. Want to try that?"

Cory nodded.

Charlotte poured her a glass of water, which Cory downed quickly before heading upstairs to brush her teeth.

Charlotte took the opportunity to call Bailey and explain what had happened.

"The sheriff found Cory at her old house. She'd run there hoping to find her brother. I'm so sorry for the inconvenience and worry she caused you."

"That's no problem. I'm just relieved to hear she's safe."

Her and every other parent in Twisted Cedars, Charlotte was sure. When Cory had first been reported missing probably everyone had been worried there was a serial kidnapper on the loose.

Shortly after her conversation with Bailey, Dougal called.

"Charlotte, is Cory okay?" He sounded breathless. "I was in a chat room with Ed when she first went missing, so I didn't hear about it until now."

"Wade brought her home, safe and sound, twenty minutes ago." Charlotte ran through the explanation again.

"You must feel like you've been through hell and back."

"I'm still in hell," she reminded him. Chester had been missing now for three entire days and two nights.

"And I know you are, too," she added. "How did your last session with Ed go?"

"Brutal. He's such a bastard. He's getting a perverse thrill out of telling me his story, and it makes me crazy knowing how happy he'll be when the story is out there for everyone to read."

"Has he said anything about Chester yet?"

"No. But I'm making progress with the story. I guess that's something."

"It's more than just something, Dougal. It could be everything."

"I hope so."

She sighed, then took the phone out the back door where she could look out over the ocean. This was a view that had never failed to calm her. Until Chester disappeared.

"Are you taking a break for dinner?"

"They've ordered in Thai food here. I think I'll stay and work on my next chapter." Dougal hesitated. "Unless you need me...?"

She did need him. But how could she put herself ahead of what was best for Chester? "I'm fine now that Cory's back. You keep writing. Give me a call later, if you have the chance."

chapter fifteen

STELLA HAD COOKED many meals for Jamie and her brother over the years, she and Amos were like the grandparents Jamie had never had, so tonight Jamie wanted to prepare something really special in return. Knowing Stella loved Mexican food, she decided on baked chicken with mole sauce, black beans and rice, and a citrus avocado salad.

It was enjoyable to putter around her brand new kitchen. Having spent most of her life in a park-model trailer with her mother—as well as Dougal, until he turned eighteen and moved to New York—the amount of counter and cupboard space seemed shockingly extravagant.

In truth, her new home was modest by modern standards. Certainly smaller than the house she'd briefly shared with Kyle and the twins after her marriage.

But those months had passed by so quickly, they almost didn't feel real anymore.

Within a few months the annulment would be finalized. And then, legally speaking, it would be like her marriage had never truly happened.

It was time she thought about what she wanted next. It was too soon to consider a new romance. But she might plan a trip. Their mother had never had the financial resources to take them traveling, however now that Jamie was back at the CPA firm, with prospects of becoming a partner, there was no reason she couldn't consider an excursion to South America or perhaps even Australia and Southeast Asia.

Jamie was considering these options when Stella arrived. It was shortly after six, and she'd come without her husband. She looked tired after a long day of cleaning houses, and her hands felt rough as she gave Jamie a hug.

"You look exhausted, Stella."

"It's been a long week with Liz off on holiday."

"What about Amos—is he coming later?"

As often happened when she was speaking of her husband, Stella avoided direct eye contact. "Oh, you know Amos. He said we'd have more fun if it was just girls."

Jamie was sad that Stella and Amos's relationship seemed so damaged. Stella had shared with her some of the reasons, which included an inability to have children.

Jamie was pretty certain there was more to the story than that.

She gave Stella a tour of her place, and Stella said all the right, complimentary things.

"It's such a nice evening I thought we'd eat on the back deck. Are you okay with that?"

"As long as I can sit, I'm happy anywhere."

Poor Stella. Working as a cleaning lady for all these years had taken a toll. And yet she'd always been there for Jamie or Dougal when they needed her. Jamie was glad to have the chance to wait on her for a change.

"Go out and put your feet up," Jamie instructed. "I'll be right there."

She grabbed a prepared jug of sangria from the fridge and put it on a tray with some glasses. With Dougal's help she'd moved the patio furniture she'd purchased for Kyle's porch to her new backyard deck and had added a couple of occasional tables to make a pleasant seating area.

"This is lovely, Jamie." Stella was settled into one of the cushioned chairs, her feet up on a stool as instructed.

"Next spring I'm going to fill those planter boxes with flowers. And buy a big umbrella."

"It's nice to be young and have plans."

Jamie filled two glasses with sangria, then went inside for chips and salsa. Once she was settled in the chair next to Stella's, the older woman shared some surprising news.

"Did you hear about Cory?"

Jamie's back went rigid. "What happened?"

"She's fine," Stella said quickly. "But she ran away after school, and for a while no one knew where she was."

"Oh my God. Charlotte must have been terrified. Where did she go?"

"To her old house on Fifth Avenue. Apparently she thought her brother might be hiding out there, but of course he wasn't."

"Poor Cory."

"She's such a dear little thing. No child should have to go through what she has."

"That reminds me." Jamie went inside to get the envelope Charlotte had given her. "I was talking to Charlotte today, and we were thinking about all the awful things that have been happening lately and wondering if there could be a root cause for it all."

Stella frowned. "I'm not sure it's that easy."

"Well, it seemed to us that a lot of the trouble started when my father came to Twisted Cedars to find his mother. We've all been focusing on Shirley Hammond and what happened to her. But Charlotte and I wondered if his father might have been involved, too."

"Ed Lachlan's father?" Stella repeated slowly. "Did you figure out who he was?"

"We have no idea. We did find this photo of Shirley with the boy who escorted her to her high school prom. We wondered if he might be the boyfriend who got her pregnant." Jamie slipped the old photograph out of the envelope and passed it carefully to Stella.

Stella stared at it a long while. "I do believe that's Sam Lemwick."

"From Sam's Market?" Jamie took the photo back for a closer look.

"Exactly."

"I had a part-time job bagging groceries for him when I was in high school." Sam had been a pleasant, easy-going boss. And he still insisted on giving her the employee discount when she did her shopping there—which she did on a regular basis. The prices might've been cheaper at the big-box stores, but Sam's Market was always clean and enticing. Plus Sam seemed to work almost all the time, providing not only top-notch service but a friendly smile as well.

"I didn't know he'd gone out with Shirley Hammond. Gosh, that must make him in his midseventies."

"I had no idea he was that old, either. I used to wonder

why he never married. Do you suppose Shirley broke his heart and he never got over her?"

"Shirley was a beautiful woman. She looked like an angel, but she had a very hard heart. Yes, I suppose it's possible that's what happened."

"Stella, think of it. If Sam was the father of Shirley's baby—that would make him my grandfather."

Saturday morning Jamie went around to Sam's Market thirty minutes before the regular nine-o'clock opening. The door was locked, but when she knocked it only took a few moments for Sam to let her in.

"Good morning, Jamie. I'm still closed, but of course for you I'll make an exception."

Sam was dressed in his usual pressed trousers, button-down cotton shirt, and pristine white apron. His gray hair was clipped short, and his eye glasses were eerily similar to the horn-rimmed pair he'd worn in high school.

He seemed spry and energetic as usual, but as she looked closer Jamie noted the lines on his face and the sunken jowls that betrayed his age.

"I'm not here to shop, Sam. I was hoping to talk to you for a few minutes." She glanced around the shop, wondering if any other employees had shown up for work yet. There was a cart filled with premium-brand canned soups in one aisle. Presumably Sam had been restocking when she interrupted him.

"I hope you're here to ask for a job," Sam teased. "I always said I'd hire you back in a New York minute."

"Tempting offer, Sam. But I think I'll stay with the CPA firm for now."

Sam chuckled, then noticed the way she was casing the joint. "We're alone. I'm running a pretty lean shop these days."

"Good. I wanted to ask you about something." Jamie let out a long breath, then took the photo out of her purse. "Charlotte Hammond and I were looking at some of her old family albums yesterday, and we found this."

She passed him the picture, and as he studied it, she tried to read the expressions on his face.

There were quite a lot of them. First he smiled, then he seemed to turn sad and possibly...regretful?

"Shirley was a beauty back in her day. I was beyond thrilled when she asked me to go to prom with her."

"*She* asked *you*?"

"I know. Amazing, isn't it? I had friends, but I was pretty much the dorkiest guy in our class. I'd been expecting to attend the dance solo."

Jamie took in the news with a strong sense of disappointment. "So this was your first date?"

"First and only."

She couldn't help sighing as she put the photograph away.

"What's this about anyway?"

"Sam, you must know Shirley left high school for a year to have a baby."

"There was a story concocted about a year in a posh eastern school to build up her credentials for college." He shrugged. "But yes, everyone in school knew she was pregnant."

"When Charlotte and I saw this photo we wondered if you might be the father of that baby."

Sam let out a surprised laugh. "Nope. Definitely not me."

"Do you have any idea who was?"

Sam's expression turned serious. He brushed a hand over his head as he pondered his reply. "There were rumors. This boy or that one. But no one ever owned up to it. And Shirley never breathed a word. She'd been a real sweet girl at one point. But this experience…it changed her."

"This isn't idle gossip on my part. I'm not sure if you've heard, but my father, Ed Lachlan, was Shirley's biological son. She gave him up for adoption, but when he became an adult my father tracked her down to Twisted Cedars."

"Yes, word has gotten around," Sam admitted.

"And that means whoever fathered Shirley's child is my grandfather. To be honest, Sam, I was hoping it was you."

chapter sixteen

AFTER AN EARLY morning meeting with his team, Wade asked Marnie if she'd made his travel arrangements to Sacramento.

"I've booked the flight and arranged for a rental car at the Sacramento airport. Since I know you have a bad habit of running down your cell-phone battery, I have confirmation numbers and your printed boarding pass on my desk."

"Great work." Especially considering it had been after eight last night when he'd called and told her he needed to interview Muriel Quinpool ASAP.

As they walked side by side down the corridor, Marnie updated him on a press conference she'd organized for later that afternoon.

He wished they had something positive to report, but as had been so clear in this morning's meeting, the only progress they had to show for their long hours and overtime was a growing list of places where Chester *wasn't*.

Wade nodded at each of the talking points Marnie outlined. Marnie had been working just as hard as, if not harder than, any of his deputies. And as with all of them, signs of strain were visible. Usually she was meticulous in her grooming, makeup, and dress, but today her hair was in a ponytail, her pale face had not even a trace of makeup, and she was wearing—if he wasn't mistaken—the same pants and blouse as yesterday.

"Did you get any sleep at all last night?"

"Four hours on your sofa." She gave him a weak grin before tackling the stacks of paper on her desk.

At that moment, the phone in Wade's office rang and he excused himself. Five minutes later when he returned, Frank Dunne was leaning over Marnie's desk. He said something in a low voice, then pulled back with a chuckle as Marnie waved her finger at him. "Behave yourself, Deputy!"

As soon as Dunne spotted Wade, his smirk vanished and he made a beeline back to the conference room.

Meanwhile, two pink splotches on Marnie's cheeks were rapidly spreading over her entire face.

"Was Dunne out of line just now?"

"Oh, he's harmless." She handed him the printout with his confirmation numbers and another with the boarding pass.

Wade glanced at the papers before folding them and slipping them into his pocket. "Make sure you let me know if he does anything…inappropriate."

Marnie tilted her head. "I wonder what you'd consider inappropriate."

That surprised him. "Anything that made you feel uncomfortable, I suppose."

"Or do you really mean anything that would make *you* feel uncomfortable?"

Wade felt he'd landed himself in conversational quicksand but had no idea how to extradite himself.

Marnie took his silence as an invitation to continue. "For instance, is there a rule against dating coworkers, Sheriff?"

Was it possible she would seriously consider dating Dunne? "No rule. But it's not a good idea."

"But there's no rule against it?"

"Not per se..."

Marnie stood up so she was almost right beside him. Quietly she said, "Then why don't *you* ask me out?"

Wade stared at her. He could feel heat building inside of him—some of it embarrassment. Some of it something altogether more dangerous. "Because I'm your boss."

"Is that the *only* reason?"

Wade considered the question. Women never ceased to amaze him, that was for sure. "If I don't leave now I'm going to miss my plane."

She gave him a half smile. "I guess you better go, then."

He did.

WADE TRIED NOT to think about Marnie as he drove south about an hour and a half to Crescent City, where he caught his short-haul flight to Sacramento.

Instead he focused on the questions he wanted to ask Muriel Quinpool. This was his second visit to her upscale condo this summer. His first had been in July when he was trying to establish the exact circumstances of Daisy Hammond-Quinpool's death. But though she'd been incredibly tense and nervous, Muriel hadn't deviated by as much as a word from the script Wade was certain she'd been fed by her son and her husband.

When Chester had first been reported missing, the state police had questioned Muriel at Wade's request. She'd claimed to have no idea where her grandson was or who might be responsible for his disappearance. But Wade wasn't sure whether to believe her.

Muriel had no credibility with him.

It didn't help that he simply didn't like her.

As a kid he'd found her aloof and cold, and he felt the same now.

Since she'd moved here four years ago, after divorcing Jim and leaving behind the grandchildren she'd helped raise since Kyle and Daisy's separation, she rarely saw her family. At one point it had seemed she wouldn't even attend Kyle and Jamie's wedding, and even when she did, she'd scurried back to Sacramento as soon as it was over.

The reasons behind the Quinpools' divorce had been a topic of some discussion when it happened. Wade's own parents—now happily retired in Arizona—had speculated in vain.

Wade had his own theory. He suspected the guilt of Daisy's unreported death and illegal burial had eventually become too much for her to stand. Rather than confess to the authorities, she'd opted to create a new life for herself.

Maybe she'd hoped putting distance between herself and Twisted Cedars would be enough to bring her relief.

But Wade had a feeling she was still tortured by her memories. And he dared to hope that today she would finally unburden herself.

Wade had phoned ahead, and Muriel came to the door

immaculately dressed, with her trademark strand of pearls at her throat. With a regal wave of her hand she invited him to sit at the sofa in the living room.

She had tea made and a plate of chocolate-covered shortbread on the coffee table. Wade noticed a photo of Chester was now taking center stage in the family grouping on the antique bureau.

It was all very staged—decorous grandmother doing her best to help the legal authorities find her grandson.

But studying her face, he saw anxiety, yes—concern for her grandson, no.

"You must be terribly worried about Chester," he opened. "I want to assure you we're working around the clock on our investigation."

"Jim thinks he's run away, that he's hiding out in one of the summer cottages that have been shut up for the season." As she spoke she smoothed imperceptible wrinkles from her freshly pressed skirt.

Wade took note of the rings on her fingers. While she no longer wore her wedding ring, she still owned several spectacular stones. The Quinpools had always been one of the wealthiest families in town, and she had seemed the pampered and adored wife who presided with some entitlement over the local woman's auxiliary group, among other charitable endeavors.

Had there been an ugly side to her marriage with Jim?

Or was he right, and it had been Daisy—her psychosis, her affair, her death—who had upset the perfection of Muriel's life?

"We've checked a lot of the local summer places already.

Unfortunately, so far we haven't found any trace of Chester."

"He'll eventually get tired of his little game, I'm sure."

Wade stared at her. Was she for real? "He's been missing three full days and three full nights now. He's only nine."

"I realize all of that, Sheriff. But Chester is a bright boy and mature for his age. I assume you came here on the hopes that I might have heard something from him. But as I've already told you on the phone I haven't. Seems to me this has been a waste of a trip for you." She sat in the same high-backed chair as last time and poured them both tea. "Do you take milk or sugar?"

"Black is fine."

"So what else do we have to talk about, Sheriff?"

"How about the night Daisy died?"

Muriel's hand trembled. She set down the teapot. "That is water under the bridge, Sheriff."

"I disagree. His father going to jail is the reason Chester wanted to run away."

"How do you know that?"

"He told Cory. And she told us."

Muriel's lips tightened. "If there was anything I could say to solve that problem, I would have said it months ago."

"I disagree. You withheld the truth last time I was here, and with your silence you're withholding it now."

She shot him an infuriated look. "Don't be insulting."

"I'm simply stating facts. Why didn't you tell me the reason Daisy and Kyle were fighting was because Kyle had found out about Daisy's affair with Brad Scott?"

Muriel's eyes widened.

"Yes, I know about that, Muriel. Don't you think that

was a rather key piece of information for you to leave out?"

"I don't see why it should matter."

"I bet you and Jim were really upset on your son's behalf when you heard about that, weren't you, Muriel? In fact, I wonder if it could have been Jim who shoved Daisy. Or you. Maybe Kyle took the blame to protect one of you, knowing at your ages prison would be a tough proposition."

"That is just...insane!" Abandoning her role as gracious hostess, Muriel rose from her chair and pointed to the door. "You had better leave. Right this instant."

"Aren't you tired of all the secrets, Muriel? You must have felt so guilty every time you saw Charlotte, knowing she was living in hope that her sister would return home one day, while you knew Daisy never would. That she was dead and buried on the Hammonds' own property."

Muriel's face drained of color, and she gripped the back of her chair. "Don't say those things."

"You put Charlotte through years of unnecessary pain. And now your grandson is paying the price for your family's crimes."

"That is *not* true. You twist everything you hear. I refuse to speak another word."

Wade said nothing, just stared into her eyes until she finally turned her back to him.

It seemed nothing would make this woman break. Muriel Quinpool was stronger than she appeared.

After several silent minutes, he let himself out.

chapter seventeen

"ISABEL FRASER WAS pathetic when she died. She begged, she cried, she even told me this sob story about how much her mother needed her."

Dougal didn't know what he hated the most. The sound of his father's voice or the sight of his face—especially his eyes, which Dougal had been told were so much like his own.

It was late Saturday afternoon, and Dougal had been sitting in the small back room at the sheriff's office for hours. He had his chair positioned about three feet from the computer screen. He would have preferred more distance, but Ed complained when he couldn't see his eyes.

The proximity was killing Dougal. It didn't help that he'd had less than four hours of sleep in a row since Chester went missing.

Even in the best of shape, though, he'd have trouble listening to Ed describe the murders. And Ed's heartless accounts of his victims' suffering was the worst.

Earlier that summer Dougal had driven to Medford and met Isabel Fraser's mother. Ruth Fraser was intelligent, good-humored, kind…and blind. She lived in an institution now, whereas if Isabel hadn't died, she would probably still be living with her daughter.

Isabel had been Ed Lachlan's fourth victim. Dougal had interviewed family members for all of them. And in each case he'd heard stories of heartache and loss and ruined lives.

He knew from researching his previous true-crime books that every murder created ripples of pain and misery.

But in those other cases, the pain and misery hadn't been caused by his own father.

And if his father was capable of doing those thing...what did that say about Dougal?

Ever since he'd been a kid, Dougal had been scared of the darkness within him. He wished he'd been born with his mother's sunny nature, like Jamie.

Instead, he had thoughts and urges that frightened him. The stories that popped into his head were so horrific that he'd actually avoided writing fiction because he was afraid to own up to them. He'd decided it would be safer to write true-crime books.

And it had been. Until he got that first email from LibrarianMomma.

When Dougal first delved into the librarian murders, he hadn't realized his father was responsible. Now that he knew, he wished he'd never left New York. Because there was no turning back now. He'd seen, first hand, the agony his father had wrought on the lives of his victims' loved ones. And now it was more than he could bear to see his father gloating about the suffering he'd caused.

No doubt he expected all these "details" to be included in the book.

But Dougal was at his limit. So far Ed had given him not

one bit of proof that he even had Chester. What if he was writing this book for nothing? Everyone else thought Chester was a runaway. Or the victim of a terrible accident.

He was the only one who totally believed he'd been abducted.

What if he was wrong?

"It's interesting actually strangling someone to death." Ed looked casual and relaxed, like he was discussing the process of something innocent and everyday—like changing a flat tire on a car. "They lose consciousness faster than you would think. But Isabel was different than the others. She—"

"Stop!" Dougal threw his notebook across the room. "Just shut the hell up for a while."

On the computer screen his father actually smiled. "But these are the details that will make our book special. Forensics are so detailed nowadays, the cops can piece together exactly what happened. But to know how it feels when a woman's body goes slack and then you watch the life drain out of her eyes...you have to talk to someone who was there, to the guy who did it."

"This is a game to you. You have no conception of your victims as human beings."

In a flash Ed's smile was replaced with an angry scowl. "You think my adopted parents viewed me as a human being? You think my mother viewed me as a human being?"

"Stop with the sob story. I've had enough. I quit. You're playing me for a fool. You don't have a clue where Chester Quinpool is—"

"Oh, really? Just you wait and see."

Abruptly Ed left his chair, and all Dougal could see was

the plain bedsheet. He could hear voices, however, and one of them sounded female.

Then Ed returned, tugging Chester by the arm and forcing him into the chair in front of the video camera.

"Here he is. Happy?"

Dougal could hardly believe his eyes. But it was definitely Chester, looking groggy but otherwise unharmed.

"Chester! Are you okay? Has he hurt you?"

"Dougal?" Chester peered at the screen. "Is that you? Help me. I'm—"

And then the screen went dark.

DOUGAL BOLTED FOR Wade's office only to find the door closed, an unusual occurrence. He turned to Marnie, typing at a crazy rate on her keyboard. "Is he back from Sacramento?"

"Yup. Twenty minutes ago." She didn't pause or even look up at him as she spoke. "But you'll have to wait to talk to him. He's scheduled for a press conference in thirty minutes, and right now he's on the phone with the computer experts at the FBI."

"Ed Lachlan's got him. Chester. I saw him on the computer."

Marnie stopped typing. "Oh. Oh no. You'd better go in and tell him."

But Dougal was already throwing the door open. Wade was at his desk, making notes as he listened to someone on the phone. He frowned at the interruption, but Dougal ignored him.

"Ed Lachlan has Chester. I saw him. He's alive. And—" Dougal stopped. He'd been about to say "well," but his throat had thickened over the word, and now he felt like crying.

Wade was staring at him. Though he was still holding the phone, it was no longer next to his ear. It was like he'd forgotten the person on the other end of the line entirely.

Dougal took a deep breath, pulled himself together.

"Ed was pissing me off, so I called his bluff. And I guess I made him angry, too, because he disappeared for a minute and then came back with Chester."

"And he was okay?"

"Yeah. Kind of groggy. But definitely okay."

Wade let out a ragged breath. "Okay. Good. I mean—thank God he's still alive at least. Hang on while I finish up here."

Too wired to settle down, Dougal paced the small space. He picked up the thunder egg, examined the intricate crystal interior, and then set it down again. He went to the window and looked past the highway to the cedars that grew at the park where the Rogue River met the Pacific and to the high bluff beyond.

Finally Wade ended his call. He set down the phone, then joined Dougal at the window. "Tell me everything."

"I'd been in that chat room with Ed for over two hours. I was tired and fed up. When he started talking about how wonderful it felt to strangle his victims, I snapped. I told him I was done, that he was bluffing about Chester and I wasn't playing his games anymore."

"And that's when he showed you the boy?"

"Yeah. Chester must have been close by—it didn't take long. He sat him down in the chair right in front of the computer."

"How did Chester look?"

"Not bad. He didn't have any bruises or other obvious injuries. He wasn't tied or shackled in any way—at least not that I could see. He just seemed sort of out of it. But not so much that he didn't recognize me. He even said my name. Asked me to help—" Again the words choked in his throat.

"Holy shit. It's a relief to know he's still alive. But—"

Wade glanced out at the ocean, and Dougal knew what he was thinking. "But for how long?" Dougal couldn't help adding.

Wade sighed, then picked up the notes he'd just made. "Now I really wish I had better news to report from our computer experts. But they've had no luck trying to trace the emails Ed sent you."

"I'm not surprised. My contact in New York couldn't do it, either."

"Apparently the connection has been crisscrossed around the world to such an extent that unraveling the threads isn't possible."

"I suspect Ed's using the same techniques to cover his tracks with this as well," Dougal said. "It won't help that he insists on using a different chat room every time."

"You may be right, but we've got to try. One of the FBI's experts should be here within five hours. Once I let them know Lachlan has Chester, they're going to be sending out an entire mobile task force."

That sounded good to Dougal. The more brainpower on this the better.

"At least we had a break with Chester's iPad." Wade exchanged one sheet of paper for another. "The very evening after Cory saw her brother talk with the so-called football coach, Chester downloaded something called WhatsApp."

"I've heard of it. It's a messaging app."

"Right. The techies were able to retrieve the messages, and they're sending me a transcript by email." Wade turned to his desktop computer. "Looks like I got it. I'll print it off."

Less than a minute later Marnie came in with a sheet of paper. "I assume you wanted this right away?"

As she passed the paper to Wade, their fingers touched, and then they exchanged a look.

Something had changed with these two.

The impression flashed in Dougal's mind, then vanished as he focused on the more important issue before them.

Wade held out the paper so that they could both read it.

Football_Coach_007: *It was good to meet you today. Your dad was a great quarterback in his time. I have a feeling you'll be just as good, if not better...*

A few messages in this vein followed as Football_Coach_007 worked to establish a rapport with the boy. He talked about some of the highlights from Kyle's years on the high school team—details that must have been gleaned from archives of the local newspaper, which, as far as Dougal knew, were only available at the Twisted Cedars Library.

Had Ed Lachlan actually gone into the library personally? Spoken to Charlotte directly?

He was such a master of disguise and had so much ego,

Dougal wouldn't put it past him.

Eventually Ed worked the conversation around to the point where he said he'd like to toss a ball around with Chester sometime. Chester suggested they meet after school at the park. Ed countered with the idea that they could meet at the turnoff to the trailer park.

Chester: *I'm not supposed to cross the highway.*

Football_Coach_007: *Just watch out for traffic. It's not hard.*

And so the trap had been sprung...

chapter eighteen

WHILE WADE AND Marnie hurriedly rewrote their official statement for the press conference scheduled for six o'clock, Dougal hurried over to Charlotte's place, where Deputy Field was already updating her with the latest.

The intense relief Dougal had felt at knowing Chester was alive was quickly fading. He was keenly aware that his phone hadn't buzzed with a single notification since Ed had terminated their last connection.

Dougal wasn't the praying kind. But he sure hoped Ed wasn't taking out his anger on Chester right now.

As he crossed the highway, he thought of Chester doing the same thing four days ago, on his way to meet the man he thought of as a football coach. Curious how Ed had suggested meeting by the trailer park.

It was where Dougal and Jamie had grown up, in a park model with two small bedrooms, each with its own bathroom, and a sitting area and kitchen in between. It had been cramped quarters, but their mother had done her best to keep it tidy and make it feel like a real home.

For the six years before Jamie was born, Ed had lived there, too. Dougal had few memories of those days, though, and the ones he had—like the time his father had killed his cat—weren't good.

After his father had split, Dougal had grown to hate living in the trailer park. He resented the lack of space, and he especially hated the social stigma of being a trailer-park kid. He'd been hard on his mother back then, something he regretted deeply now that she was gone. It was so unfair that she'd died of cancer so young. She'd deserved better from her life. In so many ways.

As he turned onto the walking path that led to Charlotte's beachfront home, he wondered if other people were thinking the same about him and Charlotte. That she deserved far better.

He tended to agree.

Yet every time he tried to keep his distance—for her sake—his resolve would crack.

And now certainly wasn't the time to make a break.

Dougal had to fight his way past the press that seemed to be permanently camped out on the street in front of the Hammonds' house. He threw out "No comments" like he'd been born into royalty and had had to say such things every day of his life.

Finally he found Charlotte and Cory on the back porch eating the ultimate in comfort food—grilled cheese sandwiches. The air was still warm, but there were clouds mounting in the west. He hadn't heard a weather report in some time, but it seemed they were in for a change.

He kissed the top of Cory's head, then Charlotte's lips. "Have you heard the news?"

"Deputy Field was just here. Chester is alive. That's the main thing." Charlotte glanced at Cory, and Dougal got the message.

"Alive and well," he agreed. "It is a relief to know that."

"But will that man let him go?" Cory asked.

"We hope so, honey. We have to pray that he will."

"Amen," Dougal agreed. Stealing a piece of Charlotte's sandwich, he was amazed at how good it tasted. "Delicious. Is that brie?"

"With a bit of fig jam."

"Mine is cheddar," Cory said.

"I made more of both kinds," Charlotte said. "In the kitchen."

Dougal went to the kitchen as directed, then came back with two sandwiches, a wine glass, and the open bottle of white he'd found in the fridge. After topping Charlotte's glass, he filled his own, then settled on the chair to Charlotte's left.

"So what have you ladies been up to today?"

"We played catch on the beach. Then Paige came over for a while and we played dress-up."

"My mom had a trunk full of dresses and stoles that belonged to her mother. They're really too exquisite to play with…but we couldn't resist, could we, Cory?"

"They were so pretty. Paige wanted to take her dress home, but it's an *earloom*, so she couldn't."

"Heirloom," Charlotte corrected. Carefully she asked Dougal, "And how was *your* day?"

"Eventful." He glanced at Cory. He wanted to tell Charlotte everything. But he wasn't sure how much Cory ought to hear.

Fortunately once she finished her sandwich, Cory was

immediately bored. "Can I go play computer games on my iPad?"

Charlotte patted her niece's arm. "Sure you can, honey." Once they were alone, she turned to him. "Tell me what happened."

He nodded. "I lost it when I was video chatting with Ed today. He was gloating about how it felt to murder someone—"

Charlotte gasped.

"Yeah." Dougal shook his head. "I was doing okay, and then I just snapped. I told him I'd had it, that I was done. And wouldn't you know it, he left the room, then came back with Chester. I actually saw him, Charlotte. Alive and well."

Charlotte put a hand on his knee and squeezed. Hard. "Are you sure he was okay?"

"Yes. He looked fine. He was really tired, but he recognized me right away. He said my name, and then he was asking me to help him when the screen just went...dark."

"Oh, God..."

Dougal pulled her into his arms. "I'm sorry. I hate that my father has him. But at least we know he didn't suffer an accident. Or get swept out to sea."

Charlotte swiped away a few tears. "Yes. He's alive. We have to hold on to that."

Dougal swallowed and looked away. There was too much hope in Charlotte's eyes for him to face right now.

Yes, Chester was fine now. But when had Ed Lachlan ever shown mercy to one of his victims?

EXPOSED

IT WORRIED CHARLOTTE that not once that evening did Dougal receive a summons from his father to resume working on the book. Had Ed Lachlan taken Dougal at face value when he'd said he'd had enough?

If so, what would that mean for Chester?

For the first time since her brother's disappearance, Cory decided to go to sleep in her own room. "Will you tuck me in?"

"Of course." Charlotte got up from the sofa where they'd all just finished watching an episode of *The Big Bang Theory*.

"You too?" Cory asked Dougal shyly.

Though clearly surprised, he jumped to his feet. "You bet."

Cory chose the Tintin adventure *The Crab with the Golden Claws* for her bedtime story, and Charlotte read the Tintin parts while Dougal covered all the other roles.

After thirty minutes, Cory's eyelids finally fluttered closed.

With a gentle touch, Charlotte stroked her niece's hair, then brushed her hand lightly over the tiny crease on her forehead. "Sleep tight, sweetheart." As she glanced at Dougal she was touched to see a tear in his eye.

He blinked it away with a rueful shrug. "She's a sweet kid."

After leaving the door ajar and the hall light on, Charlotte and Dougal retired to her bedroom. Dougal undressed her slowly, and she felt the oddest combination of arousal and sadness.

They made love solemnly, and Charlotte only managed to forget her troubles in the final, trembling, ecstatic moments of climax.

Breathless, she collapsed onto Dougal, loving how safe she felt as he wrapped his arms around her. Pressing her ear against his warm chest, she listened to the thudding of his heart, surely the most reassuring sound in the world, not unlike the lulling rhythm of the surf, which she could also hear through the open window.

She hoped she would drop off to sleep, and she did, only to be jolted awake a few hours later with a familiar feeling of dread. She rolled away from Dougal and glanced at the clock. Eight minutes after three.

The wind had picked up since they'd gone to bed, and her curtains were dancing wildly in the breeze. A glance at Dougal confirmed he was still asleep.

Quietly she crept out of bed, pulled on a nightgown, and then went to check on Cory. The little girl was deeply asleep, oblivious to the noise of the wind. Charlotte closed and latched her window and returned to her own bedroom.

She found Dougal reaching for his phone, which he'd left on the nightstand.

She read his disappointed expression with concern. "He hasn't emailed?"

"No."

The ball of dread in her gut grew bigger, but she crawled under the covers and when Dougal put his arm around her waist allowed herself to be drawn back into him. How could his touch make her feel so warm and secure, even at a time like this?

She didn't know the answer, but she was grateful for his presence.

And couldn't help wondering about Chester. His nights had to be filled with loneliness and fear.

She listened to the sound of Dougal's breath, waiting for the moment when he'd fallen back to sleep. Meanwhile she watched the minutes accumulate on the clock. When the display read 3:48 she whispered, "Awake?"

"Yeah."

"I forgot to tell you something. On Friday Jamie and I went through our old photo albums. We were looking for clues as to who might have been Ed's father."

Dougal's body tensed, and she rolled over to face him.

"I've wondered about that, too," he said. "Did you find anything?"

"If Shirley dated, there weren't any photos of her boyfriends. All we found was one picture of her with her prom date. But she'd had the baby years earlier, so that didn't help much."

"Who was her date?"

Charlotte told him about Sam Lemwick. "I wish he had been the father, but he laughed at the very idea. They only had the one date, and I doubt if Sam did much more than hold Shirley's hand while her father took their picture."

"I asked Ed once about his biological father. He told me to be patient."

"So you think he *knows* who it was?"

"Maybe. Or he could have been messing with me."

"We could try questioning some of Shirley's other classmates."

"Yeah. I'm not sure it matters much at this point." Dougal flopped onto his back. "I wish the bastard would email me. He's probably delaying just to torture me."

"But he will call eventually, right? I mean, he's gone to a lot of trouble to get you to write this book. He won't abandon the project easily."

"That's what I'm counting on…"

But his phone remained silent.

After staring at the ceiling for another twenty minutes, they gave up on the idea of sleep and went downstairs. Dougal made them hot tea with a generous addition of almond and orange liquors, and they settled on the outdoor chaise lounge, sharing both the wide chair and a blanket. The salty air and crashing waves grounded Charlotte, reminding her that some things in this world could still be counted on.

They sipped at their tea until it was gone, then pointed out familiar constellations as they peeked out from the shifting clouds.

"I just realized this is the longest I've ever gone without reading a novel."

"You mean the four days Chester's been missing?" Dougal asked sleepily.

"Yes. With so much empty time on my hands, I've tried several times to get into a book. But not even my favorite Jane Austens are working. I pick up a book, and I can't get past even one paragraph."

"Tintin excepted."

She jabbed her elbow lightly against his side. "That was for Cory."

"I was teasing." He sighed. "I know what you mean. The fear is too big. You can't push it aside."

"Exactly. Even when we were watching *Big Bang*, my stomach was twisting and churning so much I could hardly stand it."

Dougal put his hand over her belly. "Does it hurt most right here?"

"Yes." She took his other hand and placed it over her heart. "And here."

And then, at just that moment, Dougal's phone, resting on a nearby table, chimed.

Charlotte scooted to the edge of the seat, clutching the blanket tightly around her. "Is it him?"

"Yes."

chapter nineteen

Wednesday, April 7, 1975, Twisted Cedars Library, Oregon

THE LIBRARY BASEMENT smelled like sawdust and old books. Shirley was frightened but also furious. The minute he removed his hand from her mouth, she spit out the words that had been screaming inside her head. "You killed her!"

Ed Lachlan smiled. "Which 'her' are you referring to, Mother dear?"

Fear became terror as the import hit her. She backed away from this man—she would never again think of him as a boy—until she was stopped by the new bookshelves Amos Ward had installed last week.

Not only had Ed killed Isabel—he was going to kill her, too, unless someone stopped him.

Amos sometimes popped in to work on his handyman projects in the evening. But would he do so tonight?

"You killed Isabel Fraser," she said. "You strangled her with one of the red scarves you've been stealing from me."

God help her, how many of those scarves had she replaced since Ed Lachlan barged into her life?

Shirley realized the answer was the same as the number of snow globes she'd been collecting in her curio cabinet: four.

She wished she had those cheap souvenirs now. She would

love to hurl them at Ed's face and wipe away his evil grin.

"*It's been such a fun little game, Mother. Waiting to see how long it would take you to catch on. Yes, I killed Isabel Fraser. Made a good, quick job of it, too. Unfortunately for Elva I wasn't quite as effective with her.*"

"*Elva…?*" *Shirley couldn't think of anyone she knew with that name.*

He seemed to enjoy her puzzlement. He let her stew in it for several minutes before finally elaborating. "Her full name was Elva Mae Ayer. She lived in Roseburg. She was a librarian, of course, around your age. Not nearly as attractive. But not bad, either. She had a protracted death due to my inexperience. Lucky Mary Louise Beamish and Bernice Gilberg fared better."

Elva. Mary. Bernice. None of these names were familiar to her.

"*Why did you pick those particular women?*"

"*Pure chance. It was part of your punishment, you see. For every conference you attended, I would kill one librarian. I would hide in the basement of the main library just before closing hours and nab the first victim who stepped into my trap.*"

"*You actually killed these women. Strangled them. To get back at me?*"

"*Finally she gets it.*" *He rolled his eyes and chuckled, as if they were talking about a brainteaser.*

"*If you wanted to punish me—why not kill* me*?*"

"*And where would the fun be in that? One violent twist of the scarf, continued pressure for two full minutes, and then the game would have been over. You wouldn't have even understood what had happened. Or why.*"

Shirley held up her hands. "What is it you want from me? It's too late. I can't change what happened to you. Just as I couldn't change what happened to me."

Ed's eyes narrowed. "You dare to compare what happened to you to what I went through? Lots of schoolgirls deal with unexpected pregnancy. It doesn't wreck their lives. You had everything. Adoring parents, a beautiful home, lots of food, everything your heart desired. If you'd wanted, you could have kept me. Raised me as a Hammond."

"But I didn't. And I'm sorry. Is that what you've been waiting to hear me say?"

"Maybe it was. In the beginning. But it's not nearly enough now."

WADE SPENT MOST of Sunday meeting with the FBI. Now that they knew for certain Chester had been kidnapped, a mobile task force had been dispatched from Portland and the case was officially out of his control. But Wade and his team intended to keep looking for the boy as hard as ever.

The FBI had also agreed Dougal should continue working on his sessions with Ed and they had their experts working on tracing the chat-room connection. But given the dead end they'd hit trying to track down Ed's emails, Wade didn't hold out much hope that they'd be able to trace Ed that way, either.

At quarter past six Wade paused outside the door to Dougal's small office. He didn't want to risk interrupting a video chat with Ed. But after several moments of silence he figured he was safe, so he went inside.

Dougal was staring at the laptop, looking like hell. Unshaven, gaunt, and exhausted. Judging by the number of dirty mugs on the table, he was surviving on pure caffeine.

Wade leaned against the door. "How's it going?"

"You ever hear writers talk about killer deadlines? This one really is."

"I'm glad you still have your sense of humor."

"I get flashes of it now and then. Wish I could say the same for my sense of humanity."

"You've written true-crime books your entire career. This is what you do."

Dougal raised his eyebrows, and Wade said nothing more. This case was different, and they both knew it.

"You've been locked away in this room for twelve hours," Wade said. "Let's head over to the Buttermilk Café for one of their all-day breakfasts."

Dougal shook his head. "I can't stop for that long."

"Correction. You *need* to stop for that long. Come on—it's an order."

"I wasn't aware I was working for the sheriff's office these days."

"You may not be on the payroll, but you're definitely on my turf." Wade clasped a hand on Dougal's shoulder and waited while he shut down the computer.

They paused on their way out the main door, both instinctively looking up to check out the changing weather. High wispy clouds and a persistent wind from the southwest signaled a low-pressure system moving in.

At the café they both ordered the Rogue Breakfast. Instead of coffee, Wade opted for water, while Dougal ordered both.

"Your gut must be a mess with all the java you've been drinking."

"I'll go on a health-food cleanse when this is over," Dougal promised.

Wade grimaced. Not for him, thanks. "I know you're working on this book as fast as you can. I'd like to find Ed's hideout before you finish."

"That would be great," Dougal agreed. "But you do realize he may not even be in Oregon."

"Maybe not. But if he's in my county, I want to be the one who finds him."

"Is this a pissing match between you and the Feds?"

"Not at all. They've got their areas of expertise, and I've got mine."

"Well, I wish I could help you. But Ed's given away nothing since he let me see Chester."

"I was hoping maybe you'd seen something or maybe even heard something in the background."

"Christ!"

The server who was arriving with their plates of food almost dropped the plates.

Dougal glanced at the woman and apologized. He waited until she'd set down the dishes and scurried away before resuming more quietly. "I can't believe I forgot to tell you, but I did hear something. Sounded like a woman talking in the background when Ed went to get Chester."

"A woman. So they're not alone?"

"Could have been a voice on a TV program or something, but I don't think so."

"Could you tell if it was an older woman or younger?"

"Didn't sound too old. But not young, either. Sorry I can't be more helpful."

"Do you think it's possible Ed has a new girlfriend?"

Dougal grimaced. "I hope not—for her sake."

They tucked into their food for a few minutes, but Dougal quickly lost his appetite. "I keep thinking about the kid. Seeing me on the video feed probably raised his hopes about getting rescued."

That had been over a day ago. For a young boy it must've felt like an eternity. Wade pulled out his card to cover the meal. It was time they got back to work.

DOUGAL WAS IN Wade's office filling in some necessary paperwork when Marnie came to the door. "Charlotte Hammond's here to see Dougal."

Dougal raised his eyebrows at Wade, wondering if he'd called her, but Wade just shrugged. "Show her in."

A moment later Charlotte appeared with her hair in a messy bun. She was wearing skinny jeans and a baggy blue sweater with a wide neck that threatened to slide off one of her narrow shoulders. The librarian had no idea how sexy she was, which made her only more appealing. Dougal wanted to kiss every inch of her long, pale neck.

Which probably wouldn't impress Wade very much.

So he kissed her on the lips instead. "What's up?"

"I had an idea how I could help. Before you ask, the house isn't empty—Jamie agreed to hang out and work on one of her files."

"It must be hard to sit and wait," Wade said. "It may help to know that the FBI is working full throttle on this now, too."

"I'm not here to complain, Wade. I appreciate all that's being done. I just want to do my part, especially now that we know for sure Ed has Chester and he won't be coming home until this book is finished."

"What is it you want to do exactly?" Dougal asked.

Charlotte straightened purposefully. "I'm going to help you with the book."

"Appreciate the offer. But I don't see how you can do that."

She pointed to a briefcase she'd left sitting outside the office door. "I brought my laptop. If you transfer over your rough pages, I can do the editing."

Dougal did not like the idea of her reading his father's story. "We don't need to bother with editing. I'm not exactly shooting for a Pulitzer here. All I want is words on the page."

"But your father might be pickier. He probably won't be impressed with grammar mistakes, that sort of thing. With my help, a few minutes after you write your last scene, I'll have the book ready…" She paused. "What does he expect you to do when it's done?"

"He hasn't told me that part yet."

Wade, who'd been listening to the exchange with interest, held up his hand. "Well, you better ask him and find out."

"I'll ask. I can't promise he'll give me an answer."

"In any case, I think Charlotte is right. It's in Chester's best interests if this book is polished and ready to go."

Dougal scowled at him. "She's already under enough stress. Last thing she needs is to read this horror story."

"Don't give Wade a hard time. He knows I'm right. Your father may have done monstrous things. But it will make me feel better to help. Please let me."

And then she gave him a wide-eyed look he had no defense against. He gave his head a shake. "I don't like it. But if you insist…"

chapter twenty

WITH MASSIVE MISGIVINGS, Dougal led Charlotte to his small room at the end of the long corridor. "Are you sure you want to do this?"

"Absolutely."

"Okay. It's probably easiest if I download the manuscript to a memory stick and give you that. We'll upload it onto your computer to make sure there are no glitches."

In less than five minutes Dougal had a copy of the book transferred to Charlotte's laptop. He packed it up in her briefcase and handed it to her. "You planning to work at home?"

She nodded.

"Okay. Just make sure Cory doesn't see this."

"Of course."

Dougal stared hard at her, wondering how she would look at him after today. She said she wanted to help with the book. But once she saw how Ed's mind worked—would that change the way she saw him?

He thought it would.

And maybe that was okay.

From the beginning he'd felt his relationship with the librarian was too good to be true, that *she* was too good to be true.

"This stuff is heavy going. Make sure you take a break if it starts to get to you."

"I'll be fine." She gave him a smile that was meant to be reassuring.

But she still hadn't read any of the material. Even Dougal, who had interviewed many murderers in the course of his career, had been taken aback by the utter lack of humanity in Ed Lachlan.

The chapters written in Shirley's point of view weren't bad. It was the others, the inside, up-close Ed chapters comprising the majority of the book, that were soul destroying.

"You need anything else?" he asked.

"Just a kiss."

"Gladly. By the way, that sweater of yours is a real turn-on."

She kissed him back so sweetly, he didn't want to let her go. But reluctantly he finally pulled away. "Guess I better sign in for another video chat session with Ed."

She nodded, her expression suddenly grave. "Could you ask if he'd let you talk with Chester again? Maybe he'd let us *both* talk to him?"

"I will definitely ask. I don't expect he'll say yes, but if he does, I'll call you." He held up his cell phone, and she nodded.

"Will you come over later to catch a bit of sleep?"

He hesitated. "I might try to work all night. We're getting close to the end."

She looked concerned. "You're driving yourself too hard.

You need at least a few hours of sleep. Promise me you'll come over, no matter how late."

"I'll text you first," he replied, sidestepping the question.

Once she was gone Dougal closed the door, feeling like an inmate being locked inside his cell. For a moment he stared at the blank computer screen, thinking back to that afternoon in his New York apartment when he'd received his first email from LibrarianMomma.

His instinct had been to delete it.

If only he'd gone with that.

Instead he'd read it. And even now he could remember it, word for word.

You don't know me. But you should. I've got a story that will be the best of your career. Back in the seventies four women were killed. Librarians. No one ever solved the cases. But I know what happened. Ever hear of Elva Mae Ayer? She was the first. Check it out, then let me know if you want the names of the others. I am here and willing to help.

Initially he'd assumed it was made-up crap by a deranged fan.

If only he'd simply deleted it and forgotten about it, as he'd done with all the other weird emails he'd received during his writing career.

But he'd started looking into it, and before he knew it, he was hooked.

Just as Ed had known he would be.

Dougal put his hands on the keyboard and pressed the Control key. Soon the screen flickered to life. He thought about Charlotte hurrying home. Soon she'd be reading the book, stepping into the very world he'd wanted to protect her from.

No sense worrying about it now.

He went into the new chat site, following the instructions in the latest email and sending an invite to LM007. Within seconds Ed responded.

As the video came into focus, Dougal realized he wasn't the only one who was getting worn down by this work. Ed was looking his age and then some. He'd stopped shaving, and his closely cropped hair was beginning to fill in with matted, gray curls. More and more he was looking like Monty, the arthritic neighbor he'd been pretending to be when they first met.

"That took a while," Ed snarled, obviously in a foul mood.

Ed was in his usual spot, in front of the white sheet. Try as he might Dougal couldn't pick up any noises in the background.

Dougal figured he'd be damned if he'd apologize. "Took a break for some dinner."

"And here I thought you were in a hurry to get the boy back."

"I definitely am. But I'm not a machine. That said, I'd like to talk to him again."

"You will. When we're done. We're getting close."

"First I need assurance he's okay."

"He's the same as before. Playing stupid games on that iPad of his and going through chips and Coke like nobody's business."

"I hope he's got more to eat than just that."

"You want me to email you his meal plan? He's *fine*.

There'll be plenty of time for chatting when our work is finished."

"About that. When exactly, and *how* exactly, are you going to set Chester free?"

Ed swore, then raised his eyes to the ceiling in a show of extreme exasperation. "First you have to finish the book and get it published on all the big internet book companies. Once I've downloaded it and made sure you wrote it just the way I told you to, then—and only then—will I make sure Chester is returned to you safe and sound."

Dougal bit back a groan. In his mind he'd imagined all he had to do was write the book. Now Ed expected him to self-publish the damn thing, something he had no experience with. Maybe it was a good thing Charlotte had offered to help after all.

Wednesday, April 7, 1975, Basement of Twisted Cedars Library, Oregon

SHIRLEY HAD NO idea how long she and Ed had been down in the basement. It felt like hours, but it might have been only fifteen minutes. He'd bound her hands behind her back with a rope and tied her feet together at the ankles. She had to stand very still, or she'd fall, which she'd already done once.

Hard to say what was worse—hitting the concrete floor without the ability to break her fall with her arms, or having him touch her as he picked her up and set her back on her feet.

Previously she'd avoided looking at him too closely, other than observing superficially that he was a ruggedly handsome man with rather intense eyes.

But now she catalogued all the familiar features and traits. The resemblance was all too obvious, right down to the timbre of his voice.

He was his father's son, all right.

And he had a plan.

***

EVERY HOUR DOUGAL spent video chatting with his father turned into at least two or three more as he transcribed the material to his computer.

This wasn't Dougal's normal writing method.

Usually, he conducted the majority of his research and prepared an overall outline—a process that took months, sometimes an entire year—before he even began to work on the first chapter.

But this project was different. It was all about getting Ed Lachlan's version of events in written form so he would let Chester Quinpool go.

Dougal didn't worry about any of the things that normally preoccupied him on his projects, like dramatic tension, pacing, or character arcs. Nor did he care about style, word choice, or sentence structure.

He just regurgitated the words as fast as he could—mindful, always, of his father metaphorically watching over his shoulder. The last thing he wanted was to sabotage his efforts to free Chester by writing something that would annoy or offend his father.

The scenes he wrote in Shirley's point of view were the

only times when he actually felt like an author, working on a story that was his, not someone else's.

He couldn't help but find himself relating to the crusty librarian. Maybe it was because he was living in her house or because she'd been Charlotte's aunt or because they had both hated Ed Lachlan.

Probably it was for all of these reasons that he felt this connection. And while it pained him to hear how Ed had delighted in torturing her, he couldn't help feeling drawn into her version of the story.

For Dougal it felt like he was in the library basement, too. A fly on the wall, watching Ed Lachlan set his vicious trap. The tension was making his head ache and his eyes blur. Dougal paused to get more coffee and only then realized it was two in the morning.

He checked his phone and found three text messages from Charlotte, begging him to take a break and come home for some rest.

Either she was handling the book better than he'd expected her to or she hadn't gotten very far into the material. Whatever the reason, he decided to take her up on her invitation.

Fifteen minutes later, he was heading for the back porch where Charlotte had a key hidden under a flowerpot when he was startled to see Charlotte herself stretched out on the oversized lounge chair. Her long blonde hair was strewn over the pale blue blanket she'd used to cover herself.

He drank in the sight of her sleeping profile. He hoped she was sleeping deeply—that she was getting a brief respite from the nightmare of the past few days.

After a few minutes he turned to admire the ocean waves sparkling in the moonlight. The rhythmic crashing sounds and the sea tang of the air reminded him of the first time he'd made love to his librarian. It had happened on this very beach. He could see the spot just beyond the sea grass, next to a huge chunk of driftwood.

He tried to imagine meeting someone like Charlotte in New York and couldn't. She belonged to this spot, and after all those years away, he'd come to believe that he did, too.

Too tired to stand anymore, Dougal pulled up a wicker chair. His plan was to sit and watch over Charlotte for a while, but then she moaned and called out his name.

"I'm here," he answered.

She shifted to the far edge of the lounger and lifted the blanket. Needing no further invitation, he slipped off his shoes and climbed in beside her.

"Nice," she murmured, tucking her body next to his. "You okay?"

"A little squished." He smiled, turning his gaze to the sky and the ever-shifting clouds. "You know there is a comfortable queen-sized bed in the house?"

"I like it out here."

From the start her fascination with the sea and the beach had intrigued him. Charlotte was a self-admitted nervous Nellie. Almost everything outside the radius of her house, the library, this beach, and her town frightened her.

Yet she saw nothing dangerous in middle-of-the-night walks on the beach or sleeping an entire night on her back porch.

"How did it go tonight?" she murmured.

"I asked to talk to Chester. No go. But Ed did tell me he'd set him free once I had the book self-published on some internet book sites. Not that I have any idea how to do that."

"I'll figure it out."

"Thanks."

Neither one of them spoke for a few moments. Dougal's exhaustion was catching up to him, but before he let sleep suck him under he had to ask one more thing. "How's Cory?"

"She and Jamie are asleep in the guest room."

So his sister had decided to stay the night. Something about that made him feel better, for some reason. Maybe it was just nice knowing he was surrounded by the people he cared about…

chapter twenty-one

A THIN BAND of sky at the horizon had turned a luminescent indigo when Dougal was startled awake by a sob from Charlotte. He tightened his grip around her. "I'm here, baby."

What else could he say? Certainly not that it was okay, because it wasn't, and it wouldn't be—not until Chester was safely home.

"Do you think Ed will really let him go when the book is finished?"

Dougal's mother and sister had often accused him of being a pessimist. Dougal hoped that in this case, they'd be proven right. Because he just couldn't imagine his father bothering. Once he had what he wanted—the published book—Chester would be expendable to him.

But he couldn't say that.

"We've got to operate on the basis that he will. Or, better yet, that the FBI will find them soon. I know they've got their best computer experts working on it."

Charlotte shifted her head so she could look him in the eyes. "The book, by the way, is incredible."

He could feel his defensive shields going up. Instinctively he shifted his gaze and drew back from her a little. "How much did you read?"

"All of it."

"You're kidding."

"It's...riveting, Dougal. I've read all your other books. Before I even knew you, I was a fan. But this. It's different."

"I'll say."

"Don't disparage. I realize you wrote this under duress. But it's so raw and powerful and intense. It's your best yet."

"Those are words I'd love to hear about any of my books but this one."

"It hasn't needed much editing at all, either."

He wasn't sure what to say. "That's good, I guess."

"It really is. It means that as soon as you've finished the last chapter I can start the process of publishing the manuscript."

"And how do we do that?" Dougal had only worked with the traditional publishing industry to date, and that process was a meticulous one that generally required almost an entire year for cover design and the editorial process of revisions, edits, and proofreading.

"I'm not sure. But I plan to figure that out today."

Charlotte pushed up to sitting. Pulling her hair away from her face into a rope that hung down her back, she looked out at the sky. Some lower clouds had pushed in from the southwest, and the smell of rain was in the air.

"Looks like our low-pressure system is finally getting the upper hand."

Dougal pulled his cell phone out of his pocket. "Christ, it's after six. I better get back to the sheriff's office."

"How about a bit of breakfast and some coffee first?"

He was going to decline, but then he thought about the greasy pastries and the gut-rotting coffee he'd find at the office. "Do you have a travel mug?"

She did. She made coffee in a French press for him, then wrapped up two blueberry muffins and gave them to him along with an apple.

Not only that, but she'd done it in the time he'd taken to grab a quick shower and change his clothes. As he was coming down the stairs, his sister crept out of the guest room where she'd been sleeping, along with Borden. Registering no surprise at seeing him, she gave him a hug.

"Cory?" He nodded at the door.

"Still sleeping," Jamie whispered.

Dougal scooped up his cat, who turned her face away as if signaling her lack of amusement at his recent long absences. He scratched her in all her favorite places, then set her down by her food bowl and opened her favorite tin of chicken stew.

Meanwhile Jamie had settled on a stool at the island. Her dark hair was a wild mess of curls, and he couldn't resist giving one of them a tug.

She batted away his hand, then accepted Charlotte's offer of a cup of coffee. "So what's the plan today?"

"I'm going back to work on the book." Dougal's gaze shifted to Charlotte. "I should finish today."

Charlotte gave him a brave nod. "And I'm going to figure out how to get a cover for the book and get it published on the internet."

"Okay," Jamie said. "How about I spend the day with Cory? Maybe take her out to play on the beach before it rains, then take in a movie in Port Orford?"

"I think that would be good for her," Charlotte concurred.

Dougal felt that he was leaving matters in good hands as he jogged through town, taking the Ocean Way walking path to Driftwood Lane, then across the highway at Second Street.

He felt a keen sense of urgency, fueled by a solid four hours of sleep and the knowledge that whatever happened next, Charlotte would be beside him.

She had read his book—all of it—and she'd still welcomed him to her bed.

Okay, her lounge chair.

But the point was people were at their most vulnerable when they slept, and if Charlotte could still let down her guard to do that with him, then the book hadn't poisoned her opinion of him.

It was unfathomable.

But for now he would accept it as a gift, to be unwrapped and examined later.

※

WADE WAS ALREADY at his desk when Dougal arrived. The sheriff looked so rough Dougal felt compelled to offer him one of the blueberry muffins, which Wade accepted gratefully.

"Came in at five," he told Dougal between bites. "Just got off the phone with the Feds. I'll give them points for persistence. They've put together a team of their very best people to work on this. Even with someone as apparently tech savvy as your father, they feel they have a shot."

"That's encouraging. But we don't have much time. I just got a message from Ed. He wants to talk in about ten minutes. We're so near the end, this could be our last conversation before the book goes live."

Wade finished off the muffin, then stood and walked Dougal out of his office. "Once you're finished writing the book, how long will it take to publish it?"

"Charlotte's checking into that today. Her guess is that we might get the book up for sale on some internet sites within twenty-four to forty-eight hours."

"That fast, huh?"

"Amazing isn't it?" As Dougal turned to head for his office, he almost bumped into Marnie.

She was still in minimalist mode—hair in ponytail, no makeup—but her face had a glow that suggested she'd at least grabbed some sleep recently. She was carrying two to-go cups from the Buttermilk Café.

"What have you got there?" Dougal asked.

She frowned but answered, "One no-fat vanilla latte and a double-shot mocha."

"You shouldn't have," Dougal teased, reaching for one.

"Believe me, I didn't." She marched past him, handing the larger cup to the sheriff and saying something in a voice too low for Dougal to hear.

Dougal had to smile. Something was cooking there for sure, and he was glad for Wade.

DOUGAL HESITATED BEFORE clicking the last button that would open the connection between himself with his father. A double shot of single malt Scotch would sure go down well now. But he was going to need all his wits about him.

He clicked the green button.

As with every other time he'd reached out to his father, he was answered right away.

Ed's voice came in first. "You there, boy? I can't see anything."

Dougal clicked the button for video, and his father's face came into slow resolution.

At one time his father had been almost classically handsome. But time and character had made their imprint, subtly distorting his eyes and his smile, giving them a sinister aspect.

In the hours since he'd seen him last, Ed's beard had filled in just a little bit more. He was wearing the same shirt as yesterday, though. When he picked up his mug of coffee, Dougal noticed his hand was shaking.

Dougal had no idea if it was stress, withdrawal, or a medical condition. Hopefully it was all three. Given the hell Ed was putting them through, it was only fair he experienced some of it, too.

"We're getting to the last chapter here, son."

As always, Dougal inwardly winced at the word "son." "I figured as much."

Ed laughed. "Guess you already know how this one ends, in broad strokes. But it's the details that make a story."

A creepy sense of déjà vu chilled Dougal's spine. He'd said something along those lines during an interview on

NPR about a year ago.

"Yeah, I heard your interview with that snooty New York book reviewer. He tried to put you down, but you showed him up real good."

It had been a tough interview, and normally Dougal would have been pleased to hear he'd come off well. But praise from Ed meant less than nothing.

And it only made him wonder how many other interviews, articles, and news clips Ed had found about him. The internet was awesome in so many ways. But it sure stripped a man of his privacy.

"How's Chester?" he asked.

"The kid is fine. Tiresome. But fine."

"Why not let him go right now? Drop him off somewhere and let us know where to find him. I'll still finish the book. I'm sure we can have it published online within a few days."

"Don't piss me off, boy. We're doing this the way I planned it. Now, do you remember where I left off yesterday?"

chapter twenty-two

Wednesday, April 7, 1975, Basement of Twisted Cedars Library, Oregon

SHIRLEY WATCHED AS *her captor pulled out the stepladder normally used to reach the very top of the bookshelves. Ed placed it very deliberately in the unfinished section of the basement. Next he removed her red scarf, tied it to a second one he'd stashed in his jacket pocket, and then draped the red silk rope over the top of the ladder.*

She'd thought he was going to strangle her, like the others. Apparently not.

Oddly, Shirley didn't feel fear. What she did feel was intensively alive, as if all her life had been a shadowy dream and this was the only real thing that had ever happened to her.

This...and the other. The act that had created this monster.

Monster. Yes. That was what he was. Not a man, but an aberration. A part of her had always known he would turn out wrong. How could he not?

"Be right back." Ed disappeared upstairs, and she'd felt a brief flicker of hope. Maybe his plan had been to scare her and he was going to leave her here all night.

But no, within five minutes Ed was back, holding a book.

He sat down a few feet away from her and leafed through

the pages. When he smiled she supposed he'd found what he was looking for.

"I know what you're thinking," he said.

She merely stood there. She'd accepted that this was his moment. He was the director and the star both. He would place her where he wanted her. Feed her lines, when and if required.

"You're thinking," he continued after a brief pause, "that this is all your fault."

He tilted his head slightly. She guessed he wanted her acquiescence. She nodded, and he looked satisfied.

"All the cruelty I suffered as a kid—that's on you, Mother. Every night I went to bed hungry. Every welt on my body. Every cruel word they hurled at me. Those were all because of you."

He began pacing, exuding the nervous energy that was building inside of him. In the dim basement lighting, his eyes seemed to be blazing brighter and brighter, as if a red-hot fire was burning at his core.

"And the women. Those librarians. They died because of you. Those murders are all on your conscience as well."

She bowed her head as he recited their names.

Elva Mae Ayer.

Mary Louise Beamish.

Bernice Gilbert.

Isabel Fraser.

He told her about their last minutes on Earth. How it had felt to squeeze away their lives, their hopes, their futures.

Tears streamed down her face as she thought of those women and their families.

And that made him angry.

"You cry for them. Women you hardly know. But when did you ever cry for me—your own son? When did you ever feel pity *for what I suffered?"*

She blinked rapidly, trying to clear her vision.

He was right. She'd never viewed him as an innocent little boy. To her he'd always been a freak. An abomination.

Could she possibly have been wrong?

She stared into his eyes. If there'd been a shred of goodness in him at the beginning, wouldn't a tiny bit of it still remain? But if it was there, she couldn't see it.

Still, she would continue to play her role and give him the words he wanted. "I'm sorry."

Crossing his arms over his chest, he said, "It's too late for that. The suffering started with you. And today it ends with you."

He held up the book so she could see the title: Forensic Pathology.

"Interesting book this. Did you know it's surprisingly difficult to kill a person by hanging?"

She couldn't help but gasp, even though the evidence was all laid out, so neatly, before her. Only now did she notice that he'd placed the ladder directly under one of the exposed rafters.

"Did you know you need to have a drop that's long enough to produce sufficient torque to break the neck? Otherwise, if the drop is too short, the subject dies of strangulation."

He stopped reading and glanced at her. "I just asked you a question."

She'd thought she was ready to accept whatever fate he had in mind for her. So why was she suddenly trembling? This outward sign of her own weakness made her angry.

"No," she said, her voice defiant. "Of course I didn't know that. Why would I know how to hang someone?"

"I didn't say you would. I think most people would have a

difficult time believing any librarian would know something like that. Which means if she wanted to kill herself by hanging, she would probably check a book to make sure she did it correctly. Am I right?"

Again he seemed to expect an answer.

"I suppose so," she said reluctantly. "Yes."

"Good. So we'll put the book right…here." He positioned it on the ground, a few feet away from the ladder. Then he stared up at the rafters.

"Fortunately this basement has a nice high ceiling. With a bit of luck the drop will be long enough."

With a bit of luck…

At one point Shirley had hoped Amos could come by to work on the basement and rescue her. But now she hoped for the opposite. Ed Lachlan was too crazy, too violent, too lacking in conscience in any degree. If Amos got in his way, she had no doubt Ed would kill him. And too many people had already died over this.

"Obviously you've been thinking about taking your revenge on me for a long time."

"Oh, Mother. You have no idea." He took the silk rope from the ladder and approached her. His expression was almost tender as he tied the deceptively soft fabric tightly around her neck.

"I'm so glad you have good taste. Silk is so much stronger than cotton or cheap synthetics."

She tried to swallow, but the knot was so tight it hurt. Ed was still close enough she could smell his breath, his hair, his skin.

Again, she was reminded of the rapes, this time of the terrible odors, the unique scent that in her mind would only ever mean suffering, guilt, and shame.

Next Ed untied her arms, then bent to remove the rope from her ankles. When her feet were free, she considered kicking him, but the anger and defiance which had sustained her for so many years was suddenly gone.

She knew she ought to fight. Even if she wasn't able to get free, she'd read enough mystery novels to appreciate the existence of bruises and cuts on her body might make the medical examiner question a verdict of suicide.

Instead, she meekly followed Ed as he pushed her toward to the ladder. Up the rungs she climbed, with him behind her. When she reached the rung second from the top, she had to cling to the rafter to keep her balance, while Ed reached over her head to secure the scarf to the same beam of wood.

He tested the knot, then, apparently satisfied, scrambled down, leaving her perched on the ladder, unable to move her head more than a few inches to either side.

"I considered forging a nice farewell note for you but decided to forgo that theatrical touch. Better to leave everyone wondering, don't you think?"

Shirley thought of her brother and his wife. A friend she'd had in college. A few of her favorite patrons at the library. There were not many people in this world who would truly miss her. And none of them would be tormented by the thought of her suicide.

In fact her brother, snob that he was, would probably do his best to cover it up.

After all, when you were a Hammond, you kept your dirty laundry hidden, whether it was a teenaged pregnancy, suicide…

Or incest.

chapter twenty-three

CHARLOTTE WAS IN her element, back at her desk at the Twisted Cedars Library. It was still closed to the public, as it had been since Chester's disappearance, but she'd decided to work from here today so she could have access to the many resources. Within a few hours she hoped to be well versed in the requirements for self-publishing a book.

She started by reading a step-by-step guide for self-publishing in the reference section, making notes as she went along.

One of the first things she had to do was get a book cover. She tried searching for *mystery book cover designers* on the net and soon had a list of five possible designers. She emailed them all explaining that she was working on an emergency rush project. Could any of them promise her a book cover within a few hours?

She was amazed when one designer came back with a yes.

Charlotte filled out information about the book title (she made an executive decision and chose a title herself) and the author. She scoured pages and pages of photo stock before choosing cover art that seemed appropriate.

Next she had to write a few paragraphs for the back cover. With her years of experience in the industry, that wasn't too hard.

By lunch time she had opened accounts with the major online book retailers.

Reading further in her guide book, she learned that once the book was ready it would need to be formatted for the book retailers—and they didn't all accept the same format. There were people you could hire to perform not only this step but the actual process of uploading the book and the cover to the platforms.

Charlotte decided yes, she would hire someone.

The next two hours were spent approaching random formatters and trying to find one who would be willing to be not just fast but also flexible, as she couldn't predict exactly when Dougal would send her his final chapter.

After ten queries, she finally got one positive response, provided she was willing to pay double the normal fee.

She was.

At two thirty that afternoon four JPEGs of book covers popped into her email. The covers looked far more professional and intriguing than she had hoped given how quickly they'd been produced. She wrote the designer back, thanking her for her work. A moment later she received the invoice, which she paid via PayPal.

It was a whole new world, she marveled. She had a book cover, and all it had taken was a few hundred dollars and about five hours.

Now all she needed was the actual manuscript.

At three in the afternoon, she finally received a brief message from Dougal with a Word document attached.

Last chapter attached, he'd typed.

Thanks, she responded, feeling there was so much more to be said. But now was not the time.

She opened the document and gave it a quick scan for formatting errors, then ran a spell-check. As she made the required corrections she resisted the lure of getting pulled into this crucial last chapter of the story. There simply wasn't time.

One day she would read the conclusion. Hopefully when Chester was safely home and all of this was behind them.

Charlotte cut and pasted the last chapter into the book document, then saved three copies. One on her laptop, the other in her Dropbox account, and a third she sent to both Dougal and herself via email.

The book was done.

She started a new message to the book formatter she'd lined up, attaching the finished manuscript as well as the high-resolution version of the book cover. She hesitated before hitting Send. This was the point of no return.

But it was also her best chance of bringing Chester home.

She hit Send and crossed her fingers. It was just after three in the afternoon.

Everything was out of her hands now.

Hopefully the person she'd hired knew what she was doing. If so, within twenty-four hours copies of *The Librarian Killer: My Father's True-Life Confessions* by Dougal Lachlan would be available for sale all around the world.

Rain was falling hard as Charlotte locked up the library. She zipped up her light jacket, wishing she'd brought an umbrella or at least a coat with a hood.

Her last message from Dougal had asked her to meet him at the Linger Longer. A drink sounded like an excellent idea, but she didn't fancy walking across the highway, then up the long block to the pub.

Besides, she felt uneasy being away from the house for so long. Jamie and Cory had left an hour ago for their movie in Port Orford, and while Charlotte had forwarded her home phone number to her cell, she still didn't like the idea of the house being vacant.

Yes it was a long shot, but what if Chester somehow managed to get free and was able to return home? She couldn't bear the thought of him walking into an empty house.

It wasn't that nice for her, either. After a mad dash through the rain, she let herself in the back door, where she hung up her sodden jacket and left her soggy trainers on the mat to dry. She wandered through the kitchen, the family room, the study, feeling a deep melancholy for all who were gone.

She paused at the cabinet where family photos were displayed. Slowly she studied each photograph in turn, starting with her great-grandparents and ending with last year's school photos of Chester and Cory.

So few of the people in these photos were still alive. Just herself and the twins.

Dying before their time seemed to be a curse for the Hammonds. Charlotte knew from family records that both her great-grandparents and her grandparents had died in their sixties.

The next generation had been even worse. Shirley had died in her midforties, while Daisy hadn't even reached thirty.

Charlotte's parents had been well into middle age before they died in the car crash, but even that was at least ten years before their time.

Why so much pain and tragedy for one family?

On the surface, the Hammonds had historically had so much. For generations they'd been the leading family of Twisted Cedars, living in this beautiful oceanfront home and managing the local bank.

Charlotte had always been proud of her family's tradition of giving back to the community. For decades her father had served as the Twisted Cedars mayor—forgoing any salary—and her Hammond great-great-grandmother was responsible for raising the funds for, and later operating, the town's library.

Now all that was left of almost a century of tradition was one adopted daughter—herself—and Daisy's two children.

Charlotte took the stairs slowly, taking the time to examine the framed photos her mother had hung above the railing. Every Christmas they'd had a photographer come to the house and take a family photograph, and they were all here, starting from the first when Daisy was a newborn.

She'd been such a cute baby, an adorable toddler, and an exceptionally pretty little girl. In all the photographs she was held by her father, who was sitting in a chair, while her mother stood behind with a hand on her husband's shoulder.

Then Charlotte entered the scene and suddenly it was her mother holding the baby and sitting, while Daisy stood beside her dad, holding his hand.

Up the stairs Charlotte progressed, to the year she'd turned four when she and Daisy had both been deemed old enough to both stand. She in front of their mother, Daisy in front of their father.

This formation continued until the final photograph, taken the year before Daisy was married.

Charlotte was so familiar with these photographs that she rarely stopped to really look at them. But today, in her sad, lonely mood, she noticed the way Daisy had changed as the years progressed. Oh, her beauty had only intensified as she became a young woman. But the inner glow that had made her practically radiate vitality as a child seemed to turn into something hard and angry as the years went on.

Could it be that the mental illness that had marred her life after the birth of the twins had actually started much earlier?

Eventually Charlotte reached the landing to the second floor. Still chilled from the rain, she decided to have a shower. Turning the water hotter than usual, she closed her eyes and let her head rest back on the tiled wall.

Charlotte had never run a marathon. But if she had, she couldn't imagine her body aching more than it did right now. Stress and lack of sleep were catching up with her big time. The pulsing water lulled her into a state of relaxation she hadn't experienced for a very long time.

She was thinking of getting out when the bathroom door opened, admitting a waft of cooler air…and Dougal.

"Hey, Char. Mind if I join you?"

She cracked open the door for him—he was already out of his clothes. She wrapped her arms around him, shivering as his cool skin pressed against her much hotter body.

"God, this feels great," he murmured as he pulled her even closer.

They kissed, and she could taste the malt of the beer he'd just had combined with the essence that was simply Dougal, the man that she loved.

There was so much to talk about, but neither said a word as they continued to embrace under the pummeling water. When Dougal finally led her out of the shower she assumed they would towel off quickly and then make love.

But the second Dougal's head hit the pillow, he was asleep.

Less than a minute later, lulled by the rain against the roof and Dougal's slow steady breathing, so was she.

CHARLOTTE AND DOUGAL slept a solid two hours before Jamie and Cory came home. Charlotte woke first, at the sound of the front door opening and closing. Gently she removed Dougal's arm from her waist, hoping to slip out of bed without disturbing him. But his eyes opened.

"What's up?"

"Jamie and Cory are back from their movie." She glanced at the time. "They must have eaten dinner out as well."

She dressed quickly in leggings and a long sweatshirt, then paused to look at him. He was sitting on the side of the bed, looking both incredibly sexy and terrifically sad.

"I wish we didn't have to rush out of bed." He raised his eyebrows suggestively.

"Me, too." She went to him, dropping a kiss onto the top of his head. His dark curls were wild after the shower, soft and fresh smelling. "You going to be okay?"

"Eventually. I suppose it's too soon for the book to have gone live?"

"I've got my laptop downstairs. I'll go check." She'd left it by the back door, near the kitchen, and she found Jamie and Cory there, too, drinking glasses of water at the island.

As soon as she saw Charlotte, Cory came to give her a hug.

It was a tight, loving hug, and Charlotte's heart swelled. She brushed her niece's hair softly from her face. "How was the movie?"

"It was funny."

"And sweet," Jamie added. "Just what the doctor ordered."

"And you've eaten? If not, I could make some waffles."

"We did have a burger after the movie. But I definitely have room for a dessert waffle. How about you, Cory?"

Cory nodded, then pulled on Charlotte's hand. "Is the book done? Will my brother be coming home soon?"

Charlotte glanced at Jamie, who gave her a sheepish shrug. Obviously she'd explained to Cory what the deal was for Chester to be released.

"Dougal finished today, and I sent the book to someone who's going to publish it on a bunch of internet book sites. We're hoping it will be ready today or tomorrow. It's probably too soon now, but I'm going to check anyway."

"I can do that for you," Jamie offered.

"Great. My laptop is in the travel case by the door."

While Jamie pulled it out and waited for it to power up, Charlotte gathered ingredients for waffles.

"I've bookmarked the various platform sites," Charlotte told Jamie. "I should still be logged in at all of them."

"Got it," Jamie said. "I'm checking the first one right now…" A moment later she sighed. "It says *still in process*."

"It hasn't been very long. They say it can take anywhere from twenty-four to forty-eight hours."

Cory groaned. "You mean we might have to wait two whole days?"

"I hope not, sweetie." This was said by Dougal as he joined the group in the kitchen. "Anyone else hungry?"

"Aunt Charlotte is making waffles."

"Awesome."

For the next hour the four of them hung out in the kitchen, taking turns spooning the batter into the waffle maker. Charlotte put out the maple syrup and bowls of chocolate chips, pecans, and sliced bananas for toppings.

When Charlotte noticed Cory stifling a yawn, she suggested it was bedtime, and Cory didn't even protest. Dougal offered to read some of the Tintin adventures to her, and he was back downstairs fifteen minutes later.

"She put up a valiant effort, but she's fast asleep."

"We're all exhausted," Jamie said. "Do you guys mind if I sleep over again?"

"We'd love it," Charlotte said. "With any luck this will be our last night without Chester."

chapter twenty-four

AT TEN THIRTY on Wednesday morning, *The Librarian Killer* went live on one of the internet book websites. Within an hour, the book was available for sale on three others. Dougal watched over Charlotte's shoulder as she opened the Report page for one of them and was amazed to see ten copies had already been sold.

"Okay. It's real. It's out there." Dougal took out his phone and composed a message to Ed.

The book is published. Already selling copies. Here's the link. He cut and pasted the link to the book page, then added, *Now live up to your end of the deal. We want Chester home and safe.*

"Did you send him the message?" Cory was sitting at the kitchen island, coloring in the states in a map of Mexico, working on homework that her friend Paige had dropped off early this morning. She was flanked by Jamie and Charlotte, both hovering protectively around her this morning.

"I just did," Dougal assured her.

Earlier Charlotte had debated sending Cory back to school today. *Time might pass more quickly for her if she was in class with her friends.*

Why don't you ask her what she would prefer? Dougal had

asked.

Please let me stay home had been Cory's answer. And Charlotte agreed that she could.

They had explained the situation as best as they could to her, trying to minimalize the danger to her brother. Dougal did not share his own grave concerns about the day's outcome. If the worst happened, they would deal with it then.

Dougal poured himself the last cup of coffee one handed as he kept an eye on his phone, waiting for Ed's response.

He was still waiting for a response ten minutes later when Wade showed up at the back door.

Charlotte invited him in, telling him not to worry about his wet shoes. The rain was forecast to last until later that afternoon. Dougal didn't view it as a positive omen.

Wade came up to him. "God, the media out there is insane today. I've got Deputy Field making sure they all keep their distance. Any news from Ed?"

While Dougal gave him a progress report on the publication of the book and his subsequent message to Ed, Jamie got up to make a fresh pot of coffee.

"I think we're going to need a lot of this today." Jamie added water to the top of the fill line.

"I hope not," Charlotte said softly.

Dougal put his arm around her shoulder, wishing he could offer her reassurance that everything was going to work out according to plan.

But the growing silence from Ed was worrying him.

About twenty minutes later, there was another knock at the back door—this time from Stella Ward, who'd arrived to do her regular housecleaning.

Dougal hoped Charlotte would send her on her way—the tension of waiting was making it very hard for him to be civil, and the more people milling around, the harder it would be. But Charlotte being Charlotte, of course she didn't do that. She invited Stella in with a caveat: "Don't worry about cleaning today. Sit down and have a cup of coffee with us."

Stella's face relaxed with relief. "Oh, thank you, dear. It's been a terrible week—in more ways than one."

"What do you mean by that?" Jamie asked, offering Stella a stool at the island.

The older woman settled down with a deep, aggrieved sigh. "Well, Chester missing. That's been the worst, obviously. But when you add Liz's unscheduled holiday—I've had to do almost double my usual workload this week."

"Where did Liz go?" Charlotte asked.

"To Portland. To help a friend who needed emergency surgery."

"Hang on," Wade said, his gaze suddenly intense. "When did Liz go to Portland?"

Dougal turned to look at Wade. Why was he asking? Did he think Liz's absence could be somehow connected to Chester's?

Stella's answer supported that theory. "That's easy to remember. She called the very same night our young man went missing. I remember trying to tell her about it, but she was very dismissive. Said something vague like, *Well, I hope he shows up soon*. And then it was like she couldn't get off the phone fast enough."

Wade's jaw tightened. "We went door to door at the

trailer park within twenty-four hours of Chester's disappearance. I personally knocked on Liz's door. She was home then."

"But why would she lie?" Stella looked puzzled. "She's never even called in sick for work before."

"Good question. I'll head over right now and ask her. By the way, you should expect more visits from the Feds today. Not sure when—just be prepared."

Wade was almost at the door when Dougal stopped him.

"There's something you should know about Liz first. This summer she told Stella, Jamie, and me a bit about her past. It turns out her father—who's dead now—had done time in jail with Ed. Apparently the men were good buddies."

"Oh my God, that's right." Jamie turned to look at Stella. "At your house that night, remember? Liz's father told her Ed was quite the storyteller. He used to talk about Dougal a lot and brag about him being a best-selling author."

"I wish to hell someone had told me this earlier." Wade's eyes narrowed as he considered the possibilities. "Do you know if Ed and Liz ever met?"

"I'm sorry—no, I don't. And I would have told you…but I only just remembered the connection now."

"You don't think Liz is actually *helping* Ed?" Charlotte sounded appalled.

"Oh, she wouldn't." Stella sounded confident. "She's a bit intense and doesn't have a lot of social graces. But she's a hard worker and an honest person. Not the sort to let anyone push her around, either."

"Maybe not in ordinary circumstances," Wade said. "But

Ed is probably armed, and he may have coerced her."

"So it's possible Chester could be in Liz's trailer right now?" Charlotte moved closer to Cory, putting an arm around her shoulders.

"It's definitely worth checking." Wade pulled out the keys to his SUV. "Hang tight here. You'll be the first to know if I find anything." Then he added an aside to Dougal: "And you let me and the FBI know if you hear back from Ed."

Dougal gave a noncommittal grunt. Whatever Ed asked him to do, he was going to do. And he doubted law enforcement was going to be part of the game plan. But maybe they'd be lucky and Wade would find Chester before it came to that.

"Should I come with you?" he asked Wade.

"You really are vying to get on the payroll, aren't you? No. Stay here and hold the fort."

Wade hadn't been gone more than a minute when Jamie let out a gasp. She pointed at the laptop. "I just pressed Refresh. Your book has now sold four hundred copies, Dougal. *Four hundred.*"

And just at that moment, Dougal's phone chimed.

"Is it him?" Charlotte asked.

He checked his phone display. "Yes."

Everyone fell quiet as Dougal opened the message and read aloud. "'I bought a copy of the book, and I've taken a look through it. It's all there. I like the cover and the title, too. You've done a good job.'"

Dougal swallowed and reached for Charlotte's hand before paraphrasing the rest: "He wants me to go to Doris's

Fish Shack. Alone."

"No." Charlotte shook her head. "If Wade was here he'd never agree to that."

"We mess with Ed, and bad things will happen. I've got to do it, Charlotte."

"At least wait to see what Wade finds at Liz's trailer."

"I agree," Jamie said.

"No," Dougal insisted. "I need you guys to trust me. We've got to follow the instructions to the letter. There's no time to waste. He said I should be there in ten minutes."

Both Charlotte and his sister were clearly not happy with his decision.

But when he glanced at Stella—who knew Ed Lachlan better than any of them—he could tell she agreed.

chapter twenty-five

Fog kept obscuring the interior of his windshield as Dougal drove to Doris's Fish Shack, windshield wipers going at half speed. He would no sooner rub off a patch so he could see than more water vapor would immediately condense to take its place. Fortunately it was a short drive.

He parked on the shoulder, across from the park, then walked along the boardwalk with the hood of his jacket pulled over his head.

He made note of the vehicles parked around him. There were only a few—a dark gray Ford Escape, a rusting pickup, and a cherry-red VW bug.

Once inside the restaurant, he shook off his jacket and hung it on a peg beside his booth.

Would Ed bring Chester in here?

Dougal chose a booth with a view of the shore, guessing it wasn't very likely that Ed would be arriving by boat. At least, as far as he knew, his father had never been one for water sports or fishing.

Setting the stage for a potentially long wait, Dougal ordered a big breakfast and coffee from Doris herself.

In her sixties, weathered, and stocky, she offered her opinion on the weather, took his order, then left him in peace.

Dougal checked his phone, which he'd placed on the tabletop to make sure he didn't miss a call or a message. No new notifications.

The restaurant had large picture windows looking out both to the ocean and to the park. He kept swiveling to take in one view, then the other.

How long would Ed make him wait?

Dougal's food hadn't even arrived when a new message alert pinged.

Meet me on the bluffs. Alone. And tell no one. If I see anyone else, especially our noble town sheriff, the boy will be going over.

Dougal's gaze shot to the high cliffs that rose above the ocean to the west. The dangerous ledge was forbidden territory for children in town, and most of it was fenced off from the park.

There had been accidents over the years and one purposeful suicide that had happened when he was in high school.

Anyone taking a jump from the bluffs could be pretty much guaranteed instant death. The twenty-five-foot drop led straight down to jagged rocks and the full force of the Pacific Ocean.

Dougal left money on the table, then picked up his phone and switched it to vibrate.

He met Doris on her way from the kitchen, carrying his plate loaded with food.

"Forgot I had another appointment." He nodded to the money he'd left. "Hope you can find someone to eat all that.

Looks delicious."

Outside the rain was falling at the same steady rate. Dougal pulled up his hood and shielded his eyes as he studied the ledge. He could see two figures from this angle—the disparity in height suggested a tall adult and a midsized kid. He couldn't discern sex at this distance, but it seemed reasonable to assume he was looking at his father and Chester.

Dougal could feel the loud, rapid thudding of his heart. And the dampness on his palms owed nothing to the rain.

What was Ed planning?

Should he have brought a weapon with him at least? But Dougal didn't own a gun and didn't know much about shooting them. If Ed's plan was to take him out, he'd probably succeed. But hopefully Dougal would put up a good enough fight so Chester could run away. This was familiar territory for the boy. Running at full clip he'd be home in ten minutes.

Dougal followed the boardwalk for a while, then veered to the left, climbing the steep and rocky incline with purposeful strides. He could no longer make out the figures of the man and the boy.

His phone suddenly started to vibrate.

Dougal paused and then, using his body to shield the display from the rain, saw that he'd received a text from Charlotte.

WHAT'S HAPPENING? ARE YOU OKAY?

He slipped the phone back into his pocket and kept progressing up the hill. The wind grew stronger with each step, and when he reached the top a gust of air pushed his hood off his head and made his eyes sting.

And then a man stepped out from the grove of trees that ringed the bluffs. It was Ed, and he was holding on to Chester's hand.

***

AS HE DROVE toward the trailer park on the east side of town, Wade reflected on how strange it was that he hadn't spent more time here as a teenager. He, Wade, Kyle, and Daisy had hung out together during whatever free time they had. They'd rotated houses, depending on which mother would best tolerate them, but they'd never gone to Dougal's.

And yeah, sure, the trailer was small, but they'd never even ridden their bikes over to the playground during the summer.

He knew now that Dougal had been ashamed he'd lived in a trailer and even more ashamed that his mother cleaned most of their homes—well, the Quinpools' and the Hammonds' anyway—for a living. Wade's mother, who had given piano lessons out of their home, had always preferred to do her own housework. Or so she'd told his father.

Since being elected sheriff a few years ago, Wade had come to know the trailer park well. Most of the residents were peaceful folk. But he'd been here a few times for domestic disturbances and a couple drug busts as well.

Back when Jamie had lived in the family trailer alone, after the Lachlans' mother died and long after Dougal had moved to New York, Wade had dropped in on her a few times to see how she was doing. So he knew exactly where to go.

Liz had purchased the trailer from Jamie just a few months ago, and nothing much seemed to have changed. From the outside, the tidy park-model home was quiet. Liz Brooks's rusted green Jeep was the only vehicle in the driveway. If she'd gone to Portland as she'd claimed, it wasn't in her own vehicle.

Wade glanced at the neighboring units, then back at this one. Liz's trailer was the only one to have all the blinds drawn. Why? There was certainly no bright sunshine that needed to be blocked out today.

Something was definitely wrong.

Wade called into dispatch to let them know where he was and to request backup from the FBI. Then he got out of his SUV and followed the worn path to the trailer. A tub of red geraniums provided a cheerful note of color in the cool, gray day.

He walked past it to the door, then leaned in close to listen.

Despite the closed windows, had the TV been on or people talking, he would have been able to hear. But all was silent.

He knocked loudly. "Sheriff's department. Open up now."

Immediately something started making a thumping sound inside the trailer. It was coming from the back. Wade heard nothing else, just the thumping.

He knocked and called out again, then pulled out his gun and broke down the door.

In the aftermath of smashing the door, the trailer was

eerily silent. Wade scanned the space looking down the sight of his Glock. The place was a mess, but no one was here.

And then the thumping started up again. From the room at the back.

On the sofa in the sitting area was a mess of pillows and blankets. In the kitchen dirty dishes covered the countertop and small table. A small hallway led past a bathroom—empty—to the closed door of what had to be a bedroom.

Wade held his ear to the door for a few moments but heard nothing beyond the thumps. Quickly he swung open the door and raised his gun.

Liz Brooks had been tied to the bed with her wrists and ankles bound tight and duct tape over her mouth. The noise he'd heard had been her feet pounding against the footboard.

Her eyes were wide as he called out her name.

"Anyone hiding in here?"

She shook her head no, but he checked anyway, in the closet and under the bed.

When he was certain this was no ambush, he went to Liz's aid, removing the tape as gently as possible before getting out his knife to saw away the trussing of tough plastic cords.

"Are you okay?"

"F-fine." She started to cough, and he grabbed her a glass of water from the kitchen. While she was drinking he checked the bedroom on the other side of the sitting area. A white sheet had been nailed on the far wall. In front of that was a small table and a chair, while the bed had been pushed to the other side of the room.

If he'd had any doubts he was in the right place, they

were gone now.

He went back to Liz, who had finally cleared her throat and was able to talk. "Ed Lachlan. He has Chester."

"Where did they go?"

"I don't know. He was driving a gray SUV. Might have been a Ford Escape."

Wade called in the information, then sat down beside Liz. "How long has he been here?"

"Ed was waiting here when I finished work on Wednesday. He'd found the spare key I keep under the geranium pot. Stupid of me, I guess."

"If I'd known that I wouldn't have had to break down your door," Wade said, hoping to lighten the mood.

"I don't care about the door. Thank you for finding me."

Relieved to see the color returning to her cheeks, Wade pressed on with his questions. "What time did you come home on Wednesday?"

"Around five. He had Chester hidden in this bedroom where I couldn't see him. I think he'd drugged him with something. He told me he had something of my father's, and foolishly I asked him what that was. The next thing I knew, he'd pulled a gun on me."

Wade felt like punching something. Preferably Ed Lachlan's face. "And he's kept you and Chester hostage here ever since?"

"Yes. I wasn't always tied up, mostly just at night. He told me if I did anything to give him away he'd shoot Chester dead, right there and then."

"You don't happen to remember the plates on that Ford Escape do you?"

"Sorry—no." And then she started to cry.

chapter twenty-six

BY THE TIME Dougal caught up to the man and the boy, they were standing about ten feet from the edge of the cliff, unprotected from the steady rain and the buffeting wind. Ed had his arm around Chester's back.

Something was wrong with Chester. He was swaying like a drunkard, and when Ed removed his supporting arm the boy sank to the ground.

"What's wrong with him?" Dougal called out over the wind.

He began to run toward them but stopped when Ed drew a gun from the pocket of his heavy-duty raincoat.

"What the hell?"

"Slow down, boy. All in due time."

Ed smiled. The asshole was enjoying this. He didn't even seem to mind the weather. The Gortex was protecting his body from the elements, but he wasn't wearing a hood, and his gray hair and beard were completely sodden.

With exaggerated patience Dougal repeated his question. "What did you do to Chester?"

"Stop fussing. Gave the boy some Special K for breakfast. He'll be fine."

Dougal suspected he wasn't referring to cereal but the

street name for ketamine. "How much?"

"Just enough to make him sleep for a bit. I know what I'm doing."

"Bring Chester to me."

"Be patient, son. I've waited a long time for this moment. It's good to see you in person finally."

"You saw me many times when you were pretending to be Monty Monroe in that apartment in New York."

"You had no idea who I was back then. This is much more satisfying."

Maybe for you. Dougal kept his wisecracks to himself. He wasn't going to screw this up by losing his cool and antagonizing Ed. If Ed wanted to pretend this was some heartfelt father-son reunion, he would let him.

"The book is going to be a big hit. It's already climbing the bestseller charts." Ed chortled. "Didn't I tell you this story would make your career?"

He was probably right. And it was a bitter pill to swallow—that this book, the one Dougal had only written under duress and with absolutely no pleasure, would end up being the book he would be most remembered for.

"I can't tell you how good it feels to finally expose those Hammonds for the sick bastards they are. I only wish John and Patricia were still alive. But at least their memories will be tainted forever."

The man was so delusional. It was true the Hammonds had not been the pillars of respectability they'd held themselves out as. But Ed had killed six innocent women and one child. And that seemed to mean nothing to him.

But Dougal wasn't here to hold Ed accountable for his

actions.

"Let me have Chester."

"I *told* you to be patient." Ed was slowly moving away from Chester and closer to the ledge. He nodded at Dougal, as if he should follow. Was Ed planning to kill him, then toss his body out to sea?

Instead of doing Ed's bidding, Dougal started toward Chester.

"Stop!" Ed pointed his gun at the boy. "I'll kill him if you move any closer."

Dougal froze. "You promised to return him unharmed."

"And I will. As long as you do as I instruct."

Dougal let his arms drop to his sides. "Okay. Instruct me."

"Just stay exactly where you are. In exactly one minute I'm going to toss this gun into the sea. At that point you will have a choice. You can either go to Chester or you can come after me."

Dougal shook his head, trying to figure out the trap because he knew his father had an angle. He always did.

"If you run to Chester, you'll give me enough time to run and escape. Don't let my age deceive you—I have kept myself in excellent physical condition. I also have the perfect strategy worked out. If you let me go now, neither you nor the law will ever see me again.

"Of course," Ed continued, "you could just push me over the cliff, too. Later you could claim it was an accident."

Dougal stared at him in horror.

"What? I can see the hatred in your eyes. Don't try to pretend you wouldn't like to see me dead and out of your life. Forever."

As Dougal stared at his father, he realized the rain had stopped. Improbably the sky had lightened enough that he could see his father's eyes. Eyes that everyone said were so like his own.

Growing up as Ed Lachlan's son he'd always felt as if he was on the precipice of a black hole. He'd been certain that if he ever tried to get inside his father's head, he'd fall right into that hole and never come up again.

But he'd been wrong. Because he'd spent the past intense week living inside his father's deepest and darkest thoughts. He'd chronicled Ed Lachlan's story, and he'd come out the other side.

Now here he was, with the man he hated most in the world, and he felt no urge to push, to kill, to obliterate.

Charlotte had spoken the words to him so many times.

Only now did he finally believe them.

You are not him.

"Throw away the gun," he challenged his father. "See what happens."

Ed gave him a nod.

And then he did it, he actually tossed his gun out into the Pacific. For just a second Dougal hesitated. But only a second.

And then he was running for Chester, scooping the boy into his arms and checking his vital signs. Only once he'd determined that his father had been telling the truth and that the boy was merely drugged into a stupor did he glance up to see where Ed had gone.

But Ed hadn't gone anywhere. He was still on the ledge.

And he was smiling.

"Katie was the only person who ever saw any good in me. She was the kindest, most beautiful woman in the world. When she asked me to leave her, it killed me. I would have never hurt her. Or you. Or your sister."

Then Ed Lachlan turned and jumped off the cliff.

chapter twenty-seven

CHARLOTTE SAT AT the kitchen table, staring out the window while Jamie and Cory emptied the dishwasher. She felt she ought to be helping, but her body and her heart felt leaden. She wished Dougal had permitted her to accompany him. He shouldn't be facing his father alone.

Outside a weak ray of sunlight broke through the clouds, turning the raindrops clinging to the blades of grass on the side lawn into a million sparkling diamonds. Was that a good sign?

And then her phone rang. She snatched it up.

"I've got Chester." Dougal sounded out of breath but okay. "He's been drugged with ketamine, but other than that he seems fine. I'd take him to a clinic, but I think it will be better for him to be home."

"Yes. Bring him home."

Jamie and Cory crowded beside her. Jamie squeezed her shoulder, while Cory whispered, "What's happening?"

"Will do," Dougal said. "See you soon."

Realizing he'd disconnected, Charlotte set down the phone and turned to her niece.

"Dougal's bringing Chester home. They'll be here soon." As she said the words, she realized she couldn't quite believe they were true.

"Oh, thank God, thank God." Jamie cried as she hugged first Charlotte and then Cory.

And then all three of them were having a big group hug. Charlotte could feel her heart expanding and at the same time becoming lighter as she shed the thousand fears and worries she'd carried the past long week.

"I'm not going to be able to believe it until I actually see him."

"Me, too," Jamie agreed.

"Let's wait outside," Cory suggested.

By the time they'd slipped on their shoes, Charlotte could hear a vehicle approaching. She linked arms with Jamie and Cory, and they went out to the porch like that, as a team. A family.

As Dougal's vehicle nosed past the media circus outside their house, suddenly Deputy Field stepped forward to clear a path for Dougal. As he swept Chester into his arms, cameras flashed and reporters shouted out questions, but Dougal ignored them all.

"Oh my God, Chester's practically comatose!" Jamie cried as Dougal came round to the back porch.

Dougal sought out Charlotte's gaze with a message she didn't understand, other than to realize that while Chester might be home, something bad had happened out there.

As Dougal lifted the boy, Charlotte reached for Chester's head, needing to touch him and reassure herself he was real. His hair was soaked through from the rain, as was the gray hoodie he was wearing.

"How much of that drug was he given?"

"Not sure. But I called 911 before I called you. Paramedics should be here shortly."

Gently Dougal set her nephew down on the chaise lounge. Cory dropped to her knees beside her brother and put her hands on his face. "Wake up, Chester."

Her brother's eyelids fluttered, then opened. Charlotte gasped when she saw his eyes were moving in rapid, jerking motions.

"It's the ketamine," Dougal murmured. "Don't worry—it's not serious."

Charlotte crouched beside her niece, touching Chester's face, the side of his neck. "You're home, Chester. You're home, and you're safe."

Jamie had run inside, and now she returned with a glass of water. Charlotte immediately tried to get Chester to drink. To her relief, when he felt the glass press against his lips, he automatically took a sip.

"Good—keep drinking, honey. It will help get rid of the drugs." As she kissed his cheek, she was dimly aware that a siren was growing progressively louder.

The next hour was mayhem. First the paramedics swarmed Chester, checking his vital signs, testing his level of consciousness, and listening to his heart and lungs.

Along with the paramedics came the FBI, and Dougal stepped aside with them for a long discussion. Once that was done with, Chester was already much improved. He asked to use the washroom, then he changed into a clean sweat suit and allowed Charlotte to towel dry and brush his hair.

Charlotte was relieved when Chester asked for something to eat. She made him his favorite toasted cheese-and-tomato sandwich and also filled a glass with milk.

"Anyone else hungry?"

But no one was. All they wanted was to be near Chester, to reassure themselves that he was truly here, home and safe. When Chester took a stool at the island, Jamie and Cory flanked him, Cory sitting so close to her twin that their shoulders touched.

Dougal, however, was hanging out in the eating alcove, watching out the window as if he was expecting someone. Charlotte couldn't tell if he was more relieved or saddened. While the paramedics were examining Chester, he'd told her about his father's suicide. She wanted to comfort him—if that was what he needed.

But she wasn't ready to let Chester out of her sight.

Chester devoured the sandwich like he hadn't eaten all day.

"Did that man give you any food?" Cory asked.

"The lady cooked regular food for us. But the man gave me chips and Cokes."

"The lady?" Charlotte asked.

"The cleaning lady," Chester elaborated.

"Liz Brooks?" Jamie prompted.

Chester nodded.

"Is that where you were? In Liz Brooks's trailer?"

"I guess so."

Charlotte glanced pointedly at both Jamie and Dougal. So Wade had been correct. But where was Liz now?

"She was nice," Chester continued. "She kept telling him to let me go. But the old guy—he said to call him Ed—he wouldn't do it."

"Did he—hurt you?" The paramedics had given her nephew the all-clear, but Charlotte needed to be sure.

"No." Chester shrugged.

"Were you scared?" Cory asked.

Chester hesitated, and his gaze dropped to the island. "The man told me he wasn't going to hurt me. But in movies, whenever the bad guys say that, they're always lying."

"Oh, honey." Charlotte couldn't stand to think of the agonies he'd suffered. She looked over to where Dougal had been standing, to thank him for all he'd done to save her nephew.

But Dougal was no longer standing by the window. He wasn't in the room, period.

WHEN DOUGAL, KEEPING vigil at the kitchen window, spotted the sheriff's SUV pulling up to the Hammond house, he quietly exited and went out to greet him.

He'd reported Ed Lachlan's suicide when he'd called 911 earlier, and he'd already given a preliminary statement to the FBI. But he figured eventually Wade would check in with them.

And now here he was.

"Hey, Dougal." Wade stepped out of the SUV looking the way Dougal felt right now—as if he'd just gone ten rounds with Rocky Balboa. "How's Chester?"

"Inside. The paramedics have checked him over, and he's doing amazingly well. Having a sandwich as we speak."

"That's a huge relief."

"It is."

Wade stopped a few feet in front of him. "I'm not sure what to say about your dad. I'm guessing you're not interested in condolences."

Dougal shook his head. "I'm having trouble processing it. Of all the ways I pictured today going down, having Ed commit suicide wasn't one of them. I'm still trying to figure out if there was some way he faked it and is now in a luxury jet headed for Costa Rica."

"No. He didn't fake anything—his body was recovered about half an hour ago. He had ID on him for Ed Lachlan, Monty Monroe, and Brian Greenway. We'll be running his prints to make sure we've got the right guy, though."

"Oh, he was my father—I have no doubt about that. But I still can't believe he offed himself. I figured he'd want to hang around and enjoy his hour of fame. Or should I say hour of notoriety."

"I guess he figured with the book out there, his legacy was taken care of."

"Yeah. I suppose so." Dougal was tempted to pull the book out of circulation right there and then. But with so many copies already sold, what was the point? The story, for better or worse, was in the public domain, just as Ed had so desperately wished.

"How about Liz Brooks? Chester just told us they were at her trailer the entire time."

"I found her shortly after I left here this morning. Ed had been holding both Liz and Chester hostage in Liz's trailer. She's okay now, but when Ed left to make the exchange he tied her up pretty tight."

"But she wasn't hurt?"

"No."

Dougal let out a long, relieved sigh. He couldn't say he liked Liz exactly. But he would have felt awful if anything had happened to her.

"But," Wade continued, "today could have ended in catastrophe. You should have called the FBI when Ed contacted you."

"Yeah. They just said the same thing."

"Or at least me."

"You're pissed—I get that. But I couldn't risk not following Ed's instructions to the letter."

Wade shook his head. "You think Ed is the first kidnapper to demand you meet him alone? We're trained to handle that crap, man."

Dougal said nothing. He didn't begrudge Wade letting off some steam. But he wasn't going to apologize for handling the situation the way he had.

"You're a stubborn bastard," Wade finally said. "But it's done. And Chester's home again. I suppose that's what matters."

"Yup." Did Wade believe if his team had been involved Ed might be alive and in custody? If so, he was too much of a gentleman to say so.

"Okay if I step inside for a few minutes?" Wade asked.

"Sure. Come on in."

Dougal led the way through to the kitchen. A tired smile softened the stern lines of Wade's face when he took in the tight cluster of family around the island.

"Hey, Chester, it sure is good to have you back home where you belong."

Dougal was surprised when instead of smiling back at the sheriff, Chester's eyes filled with tears.

Wade noticed, too. He moved closer to the boy, leaning down so they were eye level. "What's wrong, son?"

"I shouldn't be home. I should be in jail."

Dougal wondered if the kid was in shock. Or having some sort of delusion.

Charlotte inserted herself protectively between Chester and the sheriff. "Of course you shouldn't be in jail, Chester. You've just been through a terrible experience. But it wasn't your fault. You've done nothing wrong."

She tried to hug him, but Chester rejected her attempts to comfort him. "My dad's in jail because of me! I was the one who pushed my mom. Not Dad. I made her fall, and that's why she died."

At first Dougal couldn't even process what he was saying. Around him the others seemed to feel the same way.

Wade recovered first. "You're talking about something that happened when you were only two years old, Chester. You couldn't possibly remember."

"I do remember. I just didn't figure it all out until I got older." Chester plucked a piece of cotton fluff from his pant leg. "I remember them fighting that night. It was loud, and I was scared. So I got out of bed and went downstairs."

Wade glanced at Charlotte, as if seeking her permission to continue the conversation. Charlotte hesitated, then nodded.

Dougal put a protective arm around her shoulders. Her

nephew clearly had been feeling guilty about this for a long time. He needed to talk.

Wade resumed his questioning. "Who was downstairs, Chester? Your mom and dad?"

Chester nodded.

"Anyone else?"

"No."

"What else do you remember?"

"Mom was saying bad things to Dad. She was making him mad. And I got mad, too. She couldn't see me, but I ran at her and I knocked her right over."

The poor kid was trembling. Charlotte put a reassuring hand on his back, while Cory stared transfixed at her brother.

"Do you remember anything else?" Wade, to his credit, sounded as calm as if they were discussing the recent change in the weather.

"There was a lot of blood. Grandma and Grandpa came downstairs. They talked for a while, and then Dad told me Mom was going to be okay but that he and Grandpa had to go get her some help. Then Grandma took me upstairs. She said I had to stay in my room. I don't remember anything else."

For a long moment everyone was silent. Then Charlotte asked, "Why now, Chester? Why are you telling us this now?"

"I knew Dad didn't want me to say anything." Chester dropped his gaze to the floor. "But when I was trapped with that man I couldn't stop thinking about it. It's not fair what happened to my dad. I decided if Ed didn't end up killing me, when I got home, I better tell the truth."

chapter twenty-eight

CHARLOTTE COULDN'T BELIEVE her nephew had been keeping such a big secret for so many years. What a terrible burden of guilt for a child. As Daisy's sister, she felt nothing but sympathy for him. He couldn't have foreseen the dire consequences of his violent outburst toward his mother.

Daisy herself would be the last to blame him.

As Wade continued to question him, it became apparent that it was the discovery of Daisy's body this summer that had reawakened Chester's disturbing old memory about the night he pushed his mother. Now nine years old, he was able to comprehend that his mother hadn't been okay that night, as his father had claimed.

She'd died.

And in his mind he was to blame.

"Did you ever talk about this with your dad?" Wade asked.

Chester shook his head. "I tried. But Dad said I shouldn't worry about it. He would take care of it."

In the beginning Kyle probably thought he could. He'd grown up in this town as the golden boy. He'd excelled in so many areas, easily achieved his every desire and goal.

When tragedy struck his family, he'd probably figured the normal rules didn't apply. Not to the Quinpools.

To Wade's credit, when tears began to gather in Chester's eyes, he put an end to the discussion. "That's enough for today. Chester, you've been a very brave kid."

Chester gave a stoic nod. "Will I go to jail?"

"Absolutely not. Chester, you've done nothing wrong. Pushing your mom was an accident."

"What about my dad?"

"That's a bit more complicated." Wade glanced up at Charlotte, and she knew he was thinking of the fraud Kyle had committed and the illegal burial of Daisy's body. "But I think there's a good chance he'll be coming home a lot sooner than you expected."

Chester slipped off his stool and wrapped his arms around Charlotte.

She hugged her nephew ferociously. This was only the second time Chester had come to her for comfort. She hoped she would always be here for him when he needed her. "I love you, Chester. And Sheriff MacKay is right. You've been very, very brave."

"That's for sure." Wade patted Chester on the back, then spoke softly to Charlotte. "I'd like to go over a few more things with Dougal. Okay if we use the study?"

"Sure." She watched the two men retreat, closing the door behind them. She desperately wished she could listen in on their conversation. But she would just have to wait until later tonight for Dougal to fill her in.

Turning to Jamie and the twins, she threw out a suggestion: "Now that the rain has finally stopped...anyone up for a walk on the beach?"

"Yes!" both twins answered, and Jamie gave her an approving smile.

The walk turned out to be exactly what they all needed. Just a few deep breaths of fresh sea air helped clear Charlotte's head.

Jamie had thought to bring a football, and Chester seemed to come alive when he saw that. He went out for the long pass, then tried out his own spiral on his sister.

For over an hour they played, they ran, they laughed.

And Charlotte felt a profound joy like nothing she'd experienced before.

There was no more beautiful sound on earth than the sound of children you loved having fun.

IT WAS AFTER ten o'clock when Chester finally settled to sleep in the room he shared with his sister. Leaving the door ajar and the hall light on, Charlotte headed downstairs, anxious to talk to Dougal. She found him stretched out on the sofa in the family room, snoring softly.

Not having the heart to wake him, she went to the kitchen to open a bottle of wine. She'd barely popped the cork when he joined her, yawning and stretching.

"Sorry about that."

"Don't be. It's been an incredible roller coaster of a day."

He went to the cabinet where the wineglasses were stored and took down two. How easily he moved around her kitchen now, as if it were his second home. Charlotte couldn't help wondering about the future.

Dougal had made it clear from the start that he wasn't the marrying kind. And he definitely loved his cabin out in the forest. Moving in here with her, becoming de facto father of two children—who would be teenagers before they knew it—that was the sort of scenario she could see scaring him off forever.

Of course, if Kyle was released from prison as Wade had suggested was likely, the twins would soon be moving back with their father. The idea of getting her freedom back was not at all appealing.

They carried their glasses and the bottle back to the family room and made themselves comfortable on the sofa. Then Dougal made what seemed to her an unusual toast.

"To Ed."

She echoed the words, tapping her glass to his before taking a swallow of the pinot noir. She closed her eyes, savoring the taste and the sensation of relaxation that came with it.

"So why the toast to your dad?"

"It's strange. I spent most of my life wishing I could formally renounce him as my father. But today was a revelation for me."

"In what way?"

"Before I answer that, I'd like you to read the last chapter of the book. Unless you already have?"

She shook her head. There'd been no time. Plus, she'd been more than a little reluctant. She'd come to really admire Shirley Hammond—at least the Shirley Hammond that Dougal had resurrected in his book—and she dreaded what she knew was about to happen.

"I've got the book downloaded on my phone." Dougal pulled it from his pocked and scrolled ahead to the final scene of the final chapter.

She took the phone from him somewhat reluctantly.

"Read," Dougal prompted.

So she did.

Wednesday, April 7, 1975, Basement of Twisted Cedars Library, Oregon

SHIRLEY KNEW SHE *didn't have much time left. Maybe a few minutes, or even just seconds.*

Not for the first time it struck her how unfair life could be. Particularly for mothers. Not once had Ed expressed any anger or resentment toward his biological father. He'd never even asked her who the man was.

If he'd asked her when he first showed up on her doorstep four years ago, she wouldn't have told him. Her parents' admonitions, particularly her mother's, had been so successfully engrained. Despite her education and exposure to discourse on all manner of subjects related to women and sexual abuse, Shirley had indeed felt like the guilty party.

It was her shame. Her disgrace.

She'd lived her entire life, ever since she'd turned thirteen, believing these things.

A world that should have been opening up to her with opportunities for fun, love, and happiness had instead tunneled inward, leaving her in a sort of prison.

Shirley saw quite clearly now what she'd never fully under-

stood before.

Her life at the cottage and her devotion to her books had been her way of escaping from reality. Once she would have claimed she was merely doing what she loved.

But what if the abuse hadn't happened? What if she hadn't been forced to have a baby at age fifteen and then forced to give it up?

She might have become an entirely different woman.

For sure she wouldn't be standing on this ladder, with her own scarves tied around her neck.

Her vision blurred as tears came to her eyes. She didn't try to stop them. Someone had to cry for her, for how little her life had amounted to in the end.

She'd been a good librarian, she supposed. That was the only legacy she had to leave...

Except for him, of course.

How many more people would he hurt in his angry quest for revenge?

She prayed to God it would end with her.

And maybe, if she told him the truth, it would.

"Your father..." Her voice came out faint and raspy, but she could tell he heard her.

He froze in his spot, staring at her.

"Don't you want to know who he was?"

Ed took a step closer to the ladder, his face a convoluted mess of emotions she couldn't decipher.

"You blame me for all the misery in your life. But I was fifteen. Do you know how old your father was? Forty-one."

Ed's eyes practically popped out of their sockets, and Shirley felt an amazing sense of lightness come over her.

Never in her life had she breathed so much as a word about what had happened to her.

She'd never guessed it would feel so...liberating.

"Your father...was my father. John Hammond the first. Isn't he the one you should have hated?"

"No! You're lying!"

In a flash she realized what she had to do. She was tired of playing according to other peoples' scripts. If her life had to end, she could at least choose the moment.

And the moment was now.

Letting go of the rafter, she jumped away from the ladder. The last sound she heard was the metal crashing to the concrete floor.

Followed by her son's anguished cry.

❧

"I DON'T KNOW what to say." Charlotte handed Dougal back his phone.

She looked shell-shocked, and Dougal realized he'd made a miscalculation. He took her cool hand in his. "I thought it would be easier if you read it." But clearly he'd been wrong.

"It's just so—vile."

"I agree."

She laughed bitterly. "And I thought poor Sam was the father of Shirley's baby. How much happier everyone would have been if that had been the truth."

It would still have caused a scandal back in the fifties, but Charlotte was right—nothing was worse than incest.

"I wonder if anyone in town guessed the truth."

"I doubt it."

"Poor Shirley. Poor, poor Shirley..." Charlotte went to the cabinet where the family photo albums were kept and selected one.

Dougal expected it to be one of the older albums with pictures taken when Shirley was growing up. But it turned out to be a lot more current than that.

She opened the album to the first page. "This is Daisy on her fourteenth birthday."

Dougal studied the picture, taken at the dining room table. Daisy was sitting in front of a lavish birthday cake. Beside her was Charlotte, and standing behind them both was Daisy's father.

Dougal's senses recoiled as he realized why Charlotte wanted him to look at this particular photograph. It was hard to be sure, but it almost seemed as if John Hammond had been looking down at Daisy's cleavage.

"Jesus. Do you think your father...?" He couldn't say the rest. As Charlotte had so appropriately said earlier, it was just too vile.

"Ever since Chester was abducted, I've felt that too many bad things happened in Twisted Cedars this summer. Most of them involving our three families—the Quinpools, the Lachlans, and the Hammonds."

"You felt it couldn't be coincidence," Dougal continued, guessing where she was going with this. "And you think incest might be the cause?"

"I don't know. But I can't help wondering." Charlotte set aside the album and began pacing.

"From my research I do know that incest is one of those awful patterns that tend to be repeated in families."

"All my life I've felt so fortunate that I was adopted by a nice family like the Hammonds. I've had so much, Dougal. I wasn't just grateful for the material benefits—which were many, including this beautiful property and a free education. I really thought I was part of a fine, historical family that believed in helping others and contributing to their community."

"Everyone in town sees the Hammonds that way. Not just you." In his teen years Dougal himself had envied the Hammond girls, not appreciating at all how lucky he was to have Katie Lachlan for his mother.

"But if this is true, then it's just been a sham. What kind of man abuses his own daughter?" She shuddered. "I remember my mom telling me a girl could be *too* pretty, that it could result in attracting the *wrong* sort of attention. I never guessed she might have been referring to our *father*."

A question occurred to Dougal, and for a moment he hesitated. He didn't want to stir up trouble. But if there was one thing he and Charlotte had shared up until now, it was honesty. "Did he ever do or say anything inappropriate to you?"

"*No.*" Charlotte visibly recoiled. But then her expression turned thoughtful, and she sighed. Sinking into an armchair on the other side of the room she admitted, "Not really. But I do remember a time when my father seemed to be paying me more attention. I was in my teens. Daisy had just moved out to live with Kyle. My mom started acting really possessive, and I thought at the time it was weird, as if she was jealous of my father wanting to spend more time with me."

"But she was really trying to protect you."

"I think so..." Charlotte drew up her legs and wrapped her arms around them. "Oh, God. I just want to curl into a little ball and disappear."

Dougal brought her the glass of wine. "Drink this."

She unwound one arm and accepted the glass. After a long swallow she gave him a small smile. "You're right. Alcohol is the answer."

He tried not to grin. "Get serious. This is a shock. But what your father did, or didn't, do is his baggage. Not yours."

It took her a moment to realize what he was doing. "Throwing my words back in my face, are you?"

"Why not? They're pretty wise. As is the lovely lady who said them to me."

chapter twenty-nine

WADE WAS IN a pretty good mood when he showed up for work Monday morning, which made the letter of resignation he found on his desk extra hard to take.

"Marnie," he barked. "Get in here."

She sauntered to his door—there was no other word Wade could think of to describe the way she walked. She also happened to look fabulous. She was wearing a red dress with matching heels, and she'd done her hair and makeup. "Yes, Sheriff?"

God, the lipstick she was wearing made her mouth look so…kissable. Wade could have sworn he'd never seen her wear that shade before.

He picked up the letter and waved it at her. "What the hell is this?"

"What does it look like?"

How could she sound so calm? As if her job with the department—and *him*—meant nothing at all to her. He waved for her to come inside and shut the door. "I can see this is your letter of resignation. I just want to know why you're doing it. And why *now*?"

"Well, I wasn't going to quit when Chester was missing, was I? Not with everyone working flat out the way they were."

"You mean you've been thinking about this for a while?"

"Last month Bailey Landax approached me about coming to work for her real estate company. Ever since Quinpool Realty shut its doors they've been swamped. She needs administrative help really badly."

"So that's what you're going to do? Work for a real estate company?"

"That's right."

"But I thought you were happy here."

"I was. Until you and I had that little conversation last week."

Wade felt uncomfortably hot all of a sudden. "We had a lot of conversations last week."

"True. But only one of a personal nature."

She was smiling at him. Damn. She was actually *enjoying* this. Wade made a show of rearranging the papers on his desk. He needed a minute to gather his wits.

While he delayed, he glanced over her letter again, then read it all the way through.

"So. You're giving two weeks' notice?"

"I am."

"Which would make Friday, October first, your last day?"

"Correct."

"Fine. Then I suggest Saturday, October second, we make a date to go fishing. How's that sound?"

"Fishing?"

"Weren't you pestering me a while ago about the location of my father's secret fishing spot?"

She laughed. "I guess that's true. Fishing it is. I'll pack a picnic."

She winked at him, then did that same sauntering walk all the way out of his office. He watched, enjoying the view and thinking he'd better buy a new ice chest before their date. And maybe a nice soft blanket to go with it.

ACROSS A TABLE at the Buttermilk Café, Jamie stared into the blue eyes of the man she'd once loved. Had Kyle's good looks distracted her from seeing the character flaws her brother had warned her about? There was something about blond men with blue eyes and flawless smiles. They just looked so…wholesome.

But to be fair to herself, she hadn't been won over by looks alone. She'd been pretty wowed by his devotion to his kids as well.

Never guessing, at the time, just how far that devotion would extend.

He'd done so many terrible things—the fraud, the lies, burying poor Daisy and then lying to her family about her disappearance.

But now that she knew he'd done them to protect Chester, she just couldn't hate him anymore.

"Thanks for agreeing to see me, Jamie." Kyle's voice was subdued. Even his posture was less confident than before.

"I hadn't intended to. But after Chester dropped his bombshell, I felt we needed to talk one more time."

Kyle scooted forward to the edge of his chair. "It's so

great to be home with them again. I can't thank you—and Charlotte—enough for taking care of them while I was in prison."

"Charlotte did most of it. She's going to miss them terribly."

"They've grown very fond of her, too. We've come up with a schedule—they're going to spend every second weekend with her. And drop by the library after school instead of going to Nola Thompson's."

"And how is Chester coping? Is he having any behavioral issues? Nightmares?"

"He's been surprisingly resilient. He even seems happy about being back in school."

"If only you'd told the truth from the beginning, Kyle..."

"That's easy to say now. At the time, it seemed like the best way to protect my son. And who did I hurt, really?"

"How about Charlotte and her parents? If they'd known Daisy was dead they would have been able to mourn her properly and move on. Instead they lived in an awful purgatory of hope and despair for all those years."

"Don't talk to me about the Hammonds. They acted so high and mighty, but they were nothing but trash."

Jamie shifted uncomfortably on her chair. Charlotte and Dougal had told her they had suspicions Daisy had been sexually abused by her father. Had Kyle known about that?

"What do you mean?" she asked cautiously.

"Daisy asked me to never tell a single soul. And I haven't. But now that they're both gone, there's no point in hiding what happened. Her dad made sexual advances when she was fifteen. She told her mother, and Patricia supposedly put a stop to it."

"Why do you say *supposedly*? Did she, or didn't she?"

"Well, she laid down the law, and John never touched Daisy again. But he would give her looks and say rude things when he caught her alone. Daisy couldn't understand why her mother didn't leave him. And press charges. Instead, Patricia told Daisy she was to keep quiet and never tell anyone."

"That's so wrong. Poor Daisy. I wonder if the abuse—and her mother's cover-up—contributed to some of Daisy's problems later on in life."

"I'm sure they did. And the twins and I paid for it."

Kyle sounded so bitter, and Jamie had to admit, knowing this background, she felt less sympathy for the Hammonds than she had. "But Charlotte wasn't a party to any of that."

"No." Kyle glanced away. "I suppose that's why I tried to restrict her access to the twins. I felt like shit every time I saw her. Especially when she started talking about Daisy and asking if I'd heard anything."

"What a mess."

"Yeah." He cleared his throat. "So how about you? You moving on with your life?"

"I'm trying. I bought a cute house on Horizon Hill Road."

"That's a good area. Nice views up there. A little pricey, though."

"Colin and Ben just gave me a raise. And I'm on track to be partner soon. Ben wants to push up his retirement."

"Congratulations. I know your job means a lot to you."

"Thank you." Her *career* had been a bone of contention during their brief marriage. But none of that mattered anymore.

"And what are you doing for fun?"

"I'm hoping to do some traveling next year. I'll start with Australia and New Zealand. And if I have time, Southeast Asia as well."

"Very adventurous." Kyle's eyes filled with tears. "I'm so sorry, Jamie. I didn't appreciate you when I had you."

"I'm not sure that's true. We were both happy. Once."

He looked infinitely sad as he asked, "I don't suppose that in time you might consider...?"

"Oh, Kyle. I was crazy about you once. But never *that* crazy."

On the first Sunday in November, Charlotte held a celebration-of-life service for Daisy.

"It's time to move on," she said.

And Dougal supported her in that.

He was trying to support her in other ways, too. Spending time with the twins every second weekend, doing chores around her house...most of all helping her deal with the skeletons they'd uncovered in the Hammond family closet.

Probably the biggest sacrifice of all—for him, not Borden—had been spending less time at the Librarian Cottage.

Although, to be honest, though he still loved the isolated A-frame, he didn't feel quite the same hankering for it as he had when he first moved back.

Dougal didn't know if it was writing his father's book—which was still at the top of the best-selling charts—or his epiphany on the bluffs, but he was feeling a lot happier and optimistic these days.

Charlotte had even commented on it the other night in bed.

He'd pretended to be concerned. "Am I losing my edge?"

"If being unhappy, rude, and sometimes selfish was your edge...I'm glad you lost it."

It hurt to hear her describe him that way. But Dougal knew it was true and that over the years he'd caused pain to the people he loved the most.

If he could be granted a few do-overs, he knew how he'd use them. He'd have moved back home when his mother was diagnosed with cancer, and he'd have helped Jamie plan the funeral and been there to support her afterward, too. Maybe if he'd been living in Twisted Cedars all along Jamie never would have started up with Kyle in the first place.

Charlotte had chosen the library, of all places, to hold the memorial service. She'd asked the local Anglican priest to say a few words and to give a speech. Then she'd given a reading and invited the guests to stay and watch a slideshow of Daisy's life.

Dougal had put together the photos for that, and he'd selected the music, too.

Once Daisy had been a friend of his, and he found himself remembering times when she'd seemed disturbed and had wanted to talk.

But he'd been afraid Kyle would be jealous, and so he'd pushed her away.

There were beverages and sandwiches to snack on later. Dougal was standing next to Charlotte when Stella came to pay her respects.

"I'm sorry for everything that has happened," Stella said after giving them both a big hug. "I'm afraid Daisy was someone who needed help—and never found it."

"I agree. It's very sad." Charlotte had been battling tears all afternoon, and a few more fell then.

Stella leaned in closer. "All these years, I never said anything. But I saw things when I was cleaning that made me wonder about your father...and Daisy."

Charlotte looked from Stella to Dougal, then back again. "I've begun to have those same suspicions, Stella. And Jamie had a conversation with Kyle last month where he pretty much confirmed it."

"Evil man," Stella said. "I'm sorry—I know he was your father, but it's true."

"Yes. And unfortunately evil has a way of spreading, unless you shine a good hard light on it."

"Thankfully we have our sheriff to do that," Dougal said. Wade and Marnie had attended the celebration of life earlier but had disappeared about twenty minutes ago.

"*And* you," Charlotte insisted, giving him one of those sweet yet sexy smiles that he supposed would always make him grin back like a lovesick fool.

An hour later, most of the guests had gone, and Dougal was trying to usher the few that were left out of the door. Chester and Cory were totally bored by this point as well, and Charlotte had resorted to letting them play games on their iPads in the back office, since they were having a sleepover with them tonight.

Finally, only Amos remained, at which point Dougal registered how odd it was that the handyman should be the last one to leave. Social gatherings like this one were hardly

Amos's favorite thing.

"Thanks for coming, Amos." Charlotte gave him a hug.

When Dougal offered his hand, Amos raised his eyebrows suggestively. "Could we maybe have a minute?"

"Sure."

At Amos's insistence, Dougal stepped outside with him, at which point Amos clasped him hard on the shoulder. "I want to thank you for what you wrote in your book."

"What do you mean?"

"I supposed I should say what you didn't write. About how I stole the library fund after I reported finding Shirley's body."

Dougal sighed. "I considered putting it in. But I didn't see the point. It was a long time ago. I wish you could forgive yourself at this point. I know you've lived an honest life since then."

"Scrupulously," Amos said. "But…the bad stuff you do…it never goes away, Dougal."

"No, I don't suppose it does," Dougal agreed. Through the glass door he could see Charlotte and the twins gathering the last of the sandwiches to take home. They had plans to order pizza and watch a movie later that night.

Once the kids were asleep, he hoped to make love with his librarian. And if not tonight, maybe in the next week or two…ask her to marry him.

"But maybe the good stuff never goes away, either."

the end

Want more? Check out C.J.'s another mystery book, *Tangles on Lies*!

excerpt from Tangle of Lies

April 20, 2020

"MY NAME IS Fern. Fern Sinclair." Her voice sounded tinny and false as it echoed in the cab of the U-Haul truck, but she had to keep practicing. Get used to the name. The sound of it. The way the words felt on her tongue. It was a pretty name, at least.

The view out the windshield was not so pretty. Vast fields, flat, and soggy and dull. Mid-April was not an inspiring time to cross the prairie. The lakes, rocks, and forests of the Canadian shield had been more interesting, but she had been too tense to enjoy anything in the early days of her trip. Now, with over two thousand miles between her truck and Notre-Dame-des-Pins she could feel not just her muscles, but her mind, relaxing.

At forty-three it wouldn't be easy to start a new life. But it had to be done. In her dreams she still heard the patients moaning for water, for food, many of them steeped in their own excrement. It was how you would imagine a concentration camp. Filled with the elderly and demented.

She'd been twelve hours into an interminable shift when

a local TV station reported that the Quebec government was going to step in and take over the administration of several care homes in the province, including the one where she worked, the Maison des Quatre Saisons. In addition, the situation was so dire, the federal government was sending in the Canadian Armed Forces.

She cried when she heard the news. Thank God someone was finally going to help. By then over fifty of their residents had died of covid, and many more were gravely ill. She herself had been felled by the virus in mid-February, though she'd never been tested to confirm, she knew it was covid. She'd gone to work anyway, because there were no backup caregivers to go in her place.

As glad as she was that help was coming, she also knew the time had come for her to leave. At some point there was going to be an investigation or inquiry into what had happened, and she did not want to be there for that.

Her last act in the Maison de Quatre Saisons—or as she had started to think of it, La Maison de Morte—had been to walk silently in her rubber-soled shoes to the room of a fifty-two-year-old female suffering from early-onset Alzheimer's. The woman had been admitted two years ago and was in the final stages of her disease. Recently she'd started coughing and was now exhibiting a fever. Though she hadn't been tested, it was almost certainly covid. Over the two years she'd been living in the Maison des Quatre Saisons, this woman had only a handful of visitors. Not that it mattered now. Even patients with lots of attentive family members were dying alone. No visitors permitted.

She found the patient coughing and tossing restlessly in her bed. Her untouched breakfast, lunch, and dinner trays were stacked on the table by her bed. No one had the time to feed her, and she was too far gone to do it herself.

"Wh—hack, hack—who are you?" the woman demanded, her voice a dry rasp.

"I'm your caregiver. I've come to look after you, dear." Though she was not authorized to administer medication, she took the ibuprofen sitting in a small paper cup alongside the uneaten food and offered it to the woman along with sips from a carton of apple juice. The woman drank greedily, sloppily, juice trickling down her chin and falling to her soiled nightgown.

When the woman was finished, she went to the closet in the corner of the room and selected a pair of clean sweatpants, a warm fleece top and some socks. Then she filled a basin with warm soapy water and gave the woman a sponge bath. The patient needed a good soak in the whirlpool tub—but these days no one had time for that. As she stripped off the soiled sheets, she wished for a better mask and protective shield to protect her from the disgusting fumes.

Once the patient was settled in her clean bed, in fresh clothes, she put a glass of water within easy reach and then turned the television to a cooking show, one that the patient had seemed to enjoy in an earlier stage of her disease. "How's that, dear? Look interesting?"

A series of coughs was her answer.

She tossed the dirty linens into an overflowing laundry hamper, then turned her attention to the real purpose of her visit—the patient's closet. Stuffed into one of the patients' leather loafers—which she never wore anymore—was a slim wallet. Quickly she transferred several of the small, plastic cards into the back pocket of her uniform.

On her way out she paused for a final look at the patient. "Thank you, Fern."

She hadn't submitted a formal resignation at work, nor had she given notice to her landlord, or informed any of her colleagues or neighbors that she was leaving.

She simply rented a U-Haul and packed all her stuff into it—including the cash her father had kept in his various safe spots—under the mattress, at the bottom of the freezer, inside the flour canister. She had that plus the shockingly high balance in their joint savings account. The money had come from the sale of property he'd inherited from his father, a lifetime ago, before her mother deserted them. Her father had always insisted the money wasn't to be touched. A genuine miser, he wouldn't even let her invest it. So, it sat there while they lived on his government checks and her minimum-wage salary.

Her car, a ten-year-old Honda Civic, she sold to a neighbor's son who had just gotten his driver's license. And that was it, the last of her ties to her old life severed.

She would move west, to the mountains, use Fern Sinclair's Quebec driver's license to apply for a new British Columbia one. After that she would be able to open a bank account and apply for a credit card, all in her new name.

She tried to argue away the guilt. What constituted a bad person anyway? One wrong act? Two? Stealing the dying Alzheimer's patient's ID cards had been illegal, but had it been bad in a moral sense? Fern's identity had been lost long ago to her disease.

And now a new Fern Sinclair was born.

C. J. Carmichael's newest mystery, Tangle of Lies *– Get now!*

author's note

I always find finishing writing a series to be a bittersweet experience. Initially there's a huge relief. *I did it! The books are done!* It's exciting to know that I'm now free to dream up a new story idea, with a fresh setting, and different characters. This is the most creative stage of the writing process. Before I've made a single choice, all options are open. As soon as I make one decision (*I think I'll have a female protagonist this time*) I'm already restricting the possibilities.

But I also feel sad about leaving behind my make-believe world and the characters I've grown to love (or pity, or despise). By that point, the world in my series is almost as real as the one I live in. I've gone through these same emotions as a reader. That feeling of satisfaction as a series ends, combined with the sorrow of knowing there will be no more stories quite the same as these. I hope this is how you feel, now that you've finished *Exposed*. If so, my job as an author has been fulfilled.

If you're ready for another mystery series reading experience, I invite you to the isolated mountain town of Lost Trail, Montana and my four book, *Bitter Roots Mysteries* series. Or, if you'd like a stand-alone mystery, try my newest: *Tangle of Lies*. For information on my upcoming books, promotions and giveaways, please subscribe to my newsletter. And if you have an opinion on any of my books, please leave a review. I read and appreciate them all.

acknowledgements

Many thanks to the following people who helped with the original Twisted Cedars Mysteries and this reprint:

My original team including Linda Style, Meredith Bond, Toni Hyatt, Frauke Spanuth, former Deputy (now Sergeant) George Simpson, Sue and Greg McCormick, District Attorney Everett Dial, Mike Fitzpatrick, Kathy Eliuk, Voula Cocolakis, Lorelle Binnion, Susan Lee, Brenda Collins, Donna Tunney.

My team at Tule Publishing including Jane Porter, Kelly Hunter, Meghan Farrell, Sinclair Sawhney, Cyndi Parent, Lee Hyat, Mia Gleason, and Mandi Andrejka.

book discussion questions

1) *Exposed* begins with the disappearance of nine-year-old Chester Quinpool. Did you have an initial theory on what might have happened to him? How does that compare with what happens in the book?

2) In *Exposed* we finally get into the mind of Dougal Lachlan's father. Did learning about his past make you more sympathetic to him as a character? If not, did they help you understand his actions better? How do you feel about his ultimate fate at the end of the book?

3) Discuss how the remote Oregon setting is essential to the plot of this final book in the series. When you think of this series, is there one particular setting that is most vivid for you? If so, why do you think that is?

4) In *Exposed* Dougal's father forces him to write a true crime book about a series of murders perporated by Dougal's father. Do you think Dougal had any choice but to comply with his father's wishes? Was it ultimately a healing exercise for him?

5) How did you feel when the truth came out about Daisy's death? Do you think Jamie should have forgiven Kyle for the role he played?

6) How did you feel about the ending of the book? Were the questions you had at the end of *Buried* and *Forgotten* answered? Are there any outstanding questions you would have liked C. J. Carmichael to address in an epilogue, or perhaps in a fourth novel?

more books by C.J. Carmichael

Other Titles
Tangle of Lies

Happy Mother's Day

Letters From Grace

Bitter Root Mysteries
Book 1: *Bitter Roots*

Book 2: *Bitter Truth*

Book 3: *Bitter End*

Book 4: *Bittersweet*

The Carrigans of Circle C series
Book 1: *Promise Me, Cowboy*

Book 2: *Good Together*

Book 3: *Close to Her Heart*

Book 4: *Snowbound in Montana*

Book 5: *A Cowgirl's Christmas*

Book 6: *A Bramble House Christmas*

Book 7: *Carrigan Christmas Reunion*

Bramble House Chronicles

Book 1: *Promise Me Please, Cowboy*

Book 2: *A Merry Bramble Christmas*

Book 3: *A Baby at Bramble House*

The Shannon Sisters Series

Book 1: *A Cowboy's Proposal*

Book 2: *A Convenient Christmas Proposal*

Book 3: *A Bachelor's Proposal*

Love at the Chocolate Shop Series

Book 1: *Melt My Heart, Cowboy*

Book 12: *Sweet Dreams, Baby*

Available now at your favorite online retailer!

about the author

Bestselling author C. J. Carmichael has written over 50 novels, including *Twisted Cedars Mysteries*, *Bitter Root Mysteries* and *Tangle of Lies*. Three of her novels were nominated for the Romance Writers of America RITA Award, including *A Bramble House Christmas*. A film version of *A Bramble House Christmas* premiered as a Hallmark Mystery movie in 2017.

Married, with grown daughters and some adorable grandchildren, C. J. and her husband and their Welsh Springer, Jazz, divide their time between their home in Calgary, Alberta and the family cottage on Flathead Lake, Montana. To be the first to know about upcoming releases and promotions please sign up for her monthly newsletter on her website.

Thank you for reading

exposed

If you enjoyed this book, you can find more from all our great authors at TulePublishing.com, or from your favorite online retailer.

Made in the USA
Las Vegas, NV
04 January 2025